Just then the telephone rang.

As Catherine reached out to pick it up, there was another ring. This one was from the TV. The telephone from Cassandra's bed.

"Hello," Catherine said, just as Cassandra said it, a mere second out of synch.

At first she could barely hear the voice in her ear. It was muffled and strange, as if the speaker had something over his — or her — mouth.

Then more clearly it said, "How did you like the red rose, C.B.? The bloody red rose?"

Catherine slammed the telephone down at the same moment that Cassandra did.

Her heart pounded. The words on Cassandra's phone were the exact ones she'd heard in her own ear, delayed the length of a breath. *"How did you like the red rose, C.B.? The bloody red rose?"*

Look out for:

The Diary
Sinclair Smith

Nightmare Hall:
Deadly Attraction
Diane Hoh

Twins
Caroline B. Cooney

The Witness
R.L. Stine

The Yearbook
Peter Lerangis

Point Horror

THE WATCHER

Lael Littke

SCHOLASTIC

Scholastic Children's Books,
Scholastic Publications Ltd,
7-9 Pratt Street, London NW1 0AE, UK

Scholastic Inc.,
555 Broadway, New York, NY 10012-3999, USA

Scholastic Canada Ltd,
123 Newkirk Road, Richmond Hill,
Ontario, Canada L4C 3G5

Ashton Scholastic Pty Ltd,
PO Box 579, Gosford, New South Wales,
Australia

Ashton Scholastic Ltd,
Private Bag 92801, Penrose, Auckland,
New Zealand

First published in the US by Scholastic Inc., 1994
First published in the UK by Scholastic Publications Ltd, 1995

ISBN 0 590 55704 1

Printed by Cox and Wyman Ltd, Reading, Berks

10 9 8 7 6 5 4 3 2

Chapter 1

The hooded figure watched.

It stood there on the edge of the bluff, concealed by the thick, dark trees. It watched as Cassandra Bly came out of her hilltop mansion and danced down the wide staircase to the sleek red convertible with its top down parked on the brick driveway.

Cassandra patted the fender of the little car before she got inside. "My car," she said happily. "Mine."

It was her sixteenth birthday present from her father. He'd had it delivered the night before to the mansion where Cassandra lived with her mother and stepfather. This was the first chance she'd had to drive it.

"Mine," she whispered again as she slid in behind the steering wheel and turned the key.

The hooded figure watched as she started the

car. It saw how the car leapt forward, seeming eager to go.

Cassandra could feel the power of the little car. She laughed as it sped toward that first sharp curve on the steep downhill road. Plenty of time to brake. She waited until the last moment to press her foot on the pedal.

But there were no brakes.

Frantically Cassandra spun the steering wheel, trying to turn the car in toward the hillside. But the car wouldn't steer. It sped straight ahead.

Cassandra screamed. She was going over the edge of the hill, down, down, down through the scrub oak and tangled underbrush. The car bumped and scrunched, and Cassandra was thrown against the seat belt.

Grateful for the belt, she hung onto the useless steering wheel. Then suddenly, inexplicably, the belt broke and she was thrown from the open car. Her head struck a rock.

The screaming stopped.

Cassandra lay still. The hooded figure left its place on the edge of the bluff and came down the slope. Slowly, cautiously, it came, as if to make sure Cassandra wasn't going to wake up and recognize it.

The dark shape stood over Cassandra's battered body for a fraction of a second, then with *a gloved hand laid one single bloodred rose on her chest.*

Catherine Belmont sat on the edge of her chair, poised to run. She ignored the amused glances of the other kids in the classroom. Every second counted.

There'd been that bloody car accident the day before. All Catherine knew was that Cassandra had been rushed through the streets of Lost River in a screaming ambulance. She couldn't die. She was just sixteen, like Catherine. Too young to die.

Had she still been alive when she reached the hospital? Catherine didn't know.

"Ready?" she whispered to her friend Liz at the desk in front of her.

Liz nodded and pulled her feet together, ready to launch herself.

From across the aisle Catherine could see Kade McGregor grinning as he watched them.

"Go!" he yelled as the noon bell rang and Catherine leapt to her feet.

"Drop dead," she yelled back as she sprinted for the door, dodging around desks and other kids with Liz a half step behind her. She caught a glimpse of Mr. Thornton, the math teacher, making a chug-chug motion with his arm as she sped by.

"Give Cassandra my regards," Ikey Brotman sang out, and Marla Forbes said something about people who watched soap operas being mental pygmies.

So let them think she was goofy. She had to watch. She had to find out what had happened to Cassandra.

Before most of the kids had even separated themselves from their desks, Catherine and Liz were out on the street.

"Faster," Catherine panted.

"This is as fast as I go," Liz gasped back.

It wasn't until they were a block from the high school that Catherine realized Kade was with them, loping along easily, not even winded.

"Get lost, Kade," Catherine yelled, using up breath she needed to run.

"Forget it," Kade said. "I want to see what it is that inspires you to put your feet in gear this way."

Catherine decided not to argue. She knew from living next door to Kade for a long time that he was going to do what he was going to do, no matter what she said.

"What is it today?" Kade asked. "A wedding? A murder? Don't tell me it's the Big Smooch today! That's it, isn't it? Cassandra's first kiss!"

Catherine ignored him. He was a clod. Kade the Clod.

They were almost there. Liz had tired and fallen back a few steps. But Kade was right beside Catherine as she shot through the door of Andersen's Appliances and faced the bank of TV sets stacked up against the wall.

Every one of them was tuned in to *Lost River,* the soap opera Catherine watched. A dozen screens showed Cassandra, limp and bloody, being wheeled into the hospital by the paramedics who had rescued her. They lifted her from the stretcher onto an emergency room gurney. The bloodred rose was still on her chest where the hooded figure had placed it.

Great. She'd missed only a minute or two.

"Got them all tuned in for you, Catherine. Knew you'd be here to see this episode." Mr. Andersen, the owner of the shop, had brought a couple of chairs from somewhere and placed them in front of the TVs. He motioned for Liz, who came puffing into the store, and Catherine to sit down.

"Sorry," he said to Kade. "That's all the chairs I've got. Didn't know you'd be joining them."

"No sweat," Kade said, dropping to the floor with his back against the door frame.

Mr. Andersen positioned himself where he could see both the TV sets and the rest of the shop in case a paying customer came in, then leaned against the wall, folding his arms across his chest. "Danged shame, that accident yesterday," he commented.

Catherine nodded without taking her eyes from the dozen screens. Cassandra looked so awful. Could she possibly survive? There was blood all over her blue denim jacket and jeans.

Catherine had worn her own blue denim outfit that day.

But now Cassandra's pretty clothes were soaked with blood.

A pair of swinging doors slammed open and Dr. Wyatt came striding swiftly into the emergency area.

Dr. Carlton Wyatt, the hunk who'd just joined the staff of Lost River General Hospital. The most eligible guy in all the daytime soaps.

"Oh, wow," Catherine whispered. This was a development she hadn't even thought of. Cassandra and Dr. Wyatt!

Beside her, Catherine heard Liz cheer softly. Cassandra would be all right. Dr. Wyatt was there. He'd perform one of the miracle operations he'd become famous for, and save her.

"Sure glad he turned up," Mr. Andersen said.

Dr. Wyatt told everybody what to do. "Stat!" he barked, and nurses and interns rushed to obey his orders.

He strode over and picked up the red rose. "What's this?" he demanded.

One of the paramedics shrugged. "It was on her chest when we found her, so we brought it along. Seemed kind of odd. We thought the police might want to look at it."

Catherine leaned forward, letting herself sink into the story unfolding on the screen. Cassandra Bly. Catherine Belmont. Their initials were the same. C.B. Sometimes she felt she could slide into Cassandra's character.

Cassandra's life was a whole lot more interesting than hers, and Catherine loved to watch her, living in a mansion and having all the money she wanted for clothes and everything else. Even the little red convertible from her father, although it was trashed now at the bottom of the ravine.

Certainly she wouldn't want to be injured the way Cassandra was. On the other hand, Cassandra would be coming to any moment, and . . .

Cassandra's eyelids fluttered as she lay there on the table in the emergency room. Dr. Wyatt leaned closer. "Cassandra," he said firmly. "Stay with us, Cassandra." He handed the red rose to a nearby nurse, then he plugged his stethoscope into his ears and placed the other end on Cassandra's chest where the rose had been.

Catherine could feel her own eyelids flutter. She was there on the table, trying to focus, seeing an expanse of white coat, and then . . . then looking into Dr. Wyatt's anxious blue eyes just inches from her face while he listened to her heart.

Catherine wasn't even aware that she'd sighed aloud until she heard Kade say, *"This is what you rocketed all the way here to see?"* He sounded disgusted.

"Who asked you to come?" Catherine demanded, coming back to reality. Hard, boring reality. Kade McGregor was no trade-off for Dr. Carlton Wyatt.

"How can you watch this crap?" Kade's voice rose a few notches and he simpered, "Oh, Dr. Wyatt, I hurt so much. Do something." His voice dropped down deep and he became Dr. Wyatt. "Cassandra, you must be brave. There's one chance in two-thousand-seven-hundred-and-ninety-three that I can save you if I operate immediately." Again

Kade's voice became high-pitched. "I'll take that chance, Dr. Wyatt. Carlton. Darling. Sweetheart." Kade made a gagging sound.

Liz laughed. "That's pretty good. Maybe you should get a job writing soap operas."

Catherine stared at the screen where the camera was focusing on Cassandra's seat belt back at the accident scene. The break in it was neat with no dangling threads, except at one edge.

It had been cut almost all the way through.

Someone had cut it. Someone had done something to the car's steering and brakes, too.

Someone had tried to kill Cassandra!

Catherine stifled a gasp. Let Kade and Liz make fun of the show and of her for watching it. She *cared* about Cassandra.

Besides, she was used to Kade's nonstop teasing. He'd been that way ever since the day he'd asked her to be his date for a school dance and she'd laughed. She hadn't meant to hurt his feelings, but the thought of dating Kade, who'd been like a brother ever since Catherine had moved to Greenville when she was seven, had seemed funny.

At first he had looked as if she'd slapped him, but then he'd laughed, too, and passed it off as a joke. Ever since then he'd teased her even more than usual, and sometimes not too kindly.

But she was surprised that Liz was joining in with him. She'd thought Liz was as involved in the soap opera story as she was.

"You guys can go now," she said coldly.

"Wouldn't think of it." Kade settled back against his door frame, making himself comfortable.

Dr. Wyatt told Cassandra that he had to go scrub and that he'd see her in the operating room. She reached for his hand. He turned back, gazing deeply into her eyes, and . . .

"Well, well, well, isn't this cozy?"

Catherine didn't even have to look up to know that the voice belonged to Britny. Miss Body-to-Die-For Britny Marsh. Pain-in-the-Neck Britny who thought the sun rose and set on her.

Another voice said, *"Lost River!* I haven't seen that show for over a year. Is that Cassandra? What's happened to her?"

A deep voice. Male.

Catherine twisted her head around to look at the speaker. He was tall and lanky and wore faded blue jeans and a dark green T-shirt with a golden tiger on the front.

Up above the tiger was an absolutely great

face, with nice white teeth, a substantial nose, and amused gray eyes.

"I'm Travis Cavanaugh," he said, extending a hand down to shake Catherine's. "Glad to meet another *Lost River* watcher."

Catherine felt a jolt as she gazed up at Travis. It was almost a feeling of recognition, although she knew she'd never met him before. Or maybe it was like what had happened to Cassandra when she'd first seen Dr. Carlton Wyatt. She'd gone to her doctor's office with a sore throat. Old Dr. Stobie was out on an emergency and his new young assistant, Dr. Wyatt, walked into the examining room. There'd been a voice-over of Cassandra thinking, *This is the man I've been looking for all my life,* which was a surprise since Cassandra was tight with Weston Fremont, whom she'd more or less stolen away from Liza Calder even though she'd still been going with Dane Ransom at the time. Now here she was falling in love at first sight with Dr. Wyatt.

Not that Catherine blamed her, especially since she was feeling the same way as she looked at Travis. She felt excited, as if her life was about to change somehow.

Limply she put her hand in the one Travis

Cavanaugh was offering her. Instead of shaking it, he held it. She was aware that he was staring at her. Staring openly, with a strange look on his face. Was he feeling the same thing that Catherine was?

"Cassandra!" he said.

Slowly he pulled on her hand, lifting her to her feet. "Same hazel eyes, same brown hair," he said softly. "Even the clothes are almost the same."

Liz, Kade, and even Britny watched with interest.

Nervously, Catherine took a step backward. Travis dropped her hand and gave a short laugh. "Sorry for scaring you," he said. "But you do know how much you look like Cassandra, don't you?"

"You're kidding," Catherine said. "Me? Look like Cassandra?"

"Remember last year when Cassandra's hair was long like yours?" Travis said. He gave another little laugh, almost as if he were embarrassed. "I watched *Lost River* and all the other soaps for several months last year while I was laid up with a trashed leg after an accident. I got pretty well acquainted with Cassandra, and you look just like her."

Britny took Travis's arm. "Hey, you were going to help me pick out a CD player, remember? Lunch hour will be over if we don't get with it."

Britny didn't need to watch the show — she had a life almost like Cassandra's. Plenty of money for CD players, or clothes, and that racy little white car she owned. Britny had everything she wanted. Almost.

Travis took a couple of steps away, then looked back at Catherine. "With your hair cut short like Cassandra's, you could be her."

"Well now, wouldn't that be nice," Britny said. "They're about to kill her off, you know."

"Britny!" Travis said.

Britny smiled sweetly. "Oh, I didn't mean that the way it sounded. It's just that I read in one of those supermarket rags that the actress who plays Cassandra wants to go to Hollywood, so they're probably going to kill off her character." She turned her fake smile on Catherine. "You know I didn't mean *you* any harm." Yanking on Travis's arm, she said, "Come on, let's go."

Travis gave Catherine an apologetic grin over his shoulder as they left.

Catherine watched them go. She hadn't even had the chance to tell Travis her name. She doubted if Britny would tell him.

"Ha!" Liz said. "She didn't mean *you* any harm. Ha!"

"Her bark is worse than her bite," Catherine said. But she wondered if it really was. She and Britny had never gotten along, and now Britny hated her because Catherine had recently won a spot that Britny wanted on the cheerleading team. Tall, athletic Britny had been so sure she'd be chosen. But they'd needed somebody small, like Catherine, to top off their pyramid formation. It was about the first thing Britny had ever wanted that she didn't get.

Britny would probably be happy if something bad happened to Catherine.

"Hey." Liz was gazing thoughtfully at her. "You *do* look like Cassandra, Catherine." Reaching over, she lifted Catherine's long brown hair away from her face. "Doesn't she, Kade?"

"Dead ringer." Even Kade sounded amazed as he looked at the injured girl on the TV screen and then at Catherine.

Liz let Catherine's hair drop. "Guess it takes someone new to notice something like that. Who was that guy, anyway?"

"Just moved here," Kade said. "He's in one of my classes."

Travis Cavanaugh. Catherine's mind explored his name.

Thoughtfully, she reached up to twist a strand of her hair. It felt heavy, and hot.

Maybe she'd cut it. Like Cassandra's.

Dr. Wyatt, now in surgical green gown and mask, approached the operating table where Cassandra lay. He held a gleaming scalpel.

The scene shifted to a hospital room where a bed waited with the sheets turned back.

Catherine presumed that was where Cassandra would be taken after the operation.

A gloved hand reached out and placed a thin white vase holding one bloodred rose on the bedside stand.

Catherine shivered, almost wishing Travis Cavanaugh had not told her how much she looked like Cassandra.

Chapter 2

That second rose was more mysterious than the first. Who had put it there? Was it the hooded figure again?

Maybe it was something romantic. Maybe Dr. Wyatt had told the emergency room nurse to put the rose there. After all, he didn't know that Cassandra's car had lost its brakes and steering. He didn't know about the severed seat belt or the hooded, watching figure.

"What do you think those roses mean?" Catherine asked as she and Liz and Kade hurried back to school after the *Lost River* episode was over. They'd stopped to grab some burgers-to-go and were munching them as they jogged along.

"What roses?" Kade looked around as if Catherine were talking about something they were passing.

Catherine sighed. "The ones somebody left for Cassandra."

"Ah," Kade said. "A sinister figure. A gloved hand. Bloodred roses. You'd better not get too attached to Cassandra, Catherine. You know what Britny said." With an index finger he made a slashing motion across his throat as he sucked air in through his teeth.

Grinning, he took a big bite of his burger.

Catherine shook her head firmly. "Not Cassandra. They wouldn't do away with Cassandra. The producers of the show, I mean. I don't care what Britny said. They wouldn't kill off one of the major characters."

"Sure they would." Liz finished chewing what she had in her mouth and swallowed it. "They do it all the time. When an actor wants to go try something else, they axe the character."

"No! Not Cassandra," Catherine said. She wasn't even going to discuss it with Liz and Kade. What did they know?

Kade gave her a brief glance. "Get with it, Cath. It's only a soap opera. You sound as if you think it's real."

It *was* real, to Catherine.

They were back at the main entrance to the high school now. With a "See ya later," Kade shot off down the corridor to his math class while Catherine and Liz headed for their English class.

Catherine dumped the remains of her burger into a trash can on the way. She didn't want ketchup running down her chin in case Travis Cavanaugh should happen to pass by.

She didn't see him, but as she plopped into her seat in the classroom she recaptured the good feeling she'd had at the appliance shop. The feeling that her life was going to change. She'd known it the instant she'd looked up into Travis Cavanaugh's face. He'd meant it as a compliment when he said she looked like Cassandra. It wasn't anything to be afraid of.

She blotted out what Britny had said and thought of herself as playing a new role in the drama of her own life. A drama involving Travis Cavanaugh. That meant she'd have to take him away from Britny the way Cassandra had taken Weston Fremont away from Liza Calder.

That sure wasn't going to make Britny like her any better.

Who cared? She felt special. She, Catherine Belmont, had been chosen for a role in this new drama just as surely as if she'd auditioned for it.

She didn't know exactly what the role was,

any more than she knew what would happen the next day on the soap opera. But somewhere she'd meet Travis again, and a whole new plot line would begin, just as one was beginning for Cassandra with Dr. Wyatt.

She sat at her desk in English class, listening to the drone of Mrs. Olsen's voice and the scratching of pencils on paper and the creaking of desks as the trapped students shifted around, trying to get comfortable.

She imagined that somewhere an unseen camera was trained on her. It recorded every motion, the turn of her head, the glance of her eye, the slight frown as she concentrated on the long poem Mrs. Olsen was reading. Something by a long-dead poet named Matthew Arnold.

" 'For we are all,' " Mrs. Olsen read, " 'like swimmers in the sea, Poised on the top of a huge wave of fate, Which hangs, uncertain to which side to fall. . . .' "

"Yes," Catherine whispered. "That's it." She tipped her face so the camera could catch her look of sudden understanding, her recognition that she was on top of that huge wave of fate.

"Catherine. *Catherine!*"

Liz was poking her.

"Catherine," Liz whispered, "are you

weirding out or something? You're talking to yourself."

Catherine heard snickers around the classroom. She ducked her head, pretending to follow the lines of the poem in her book. How could she have spoken out loud?

Her cheeks felt hot. She was glad Travis wasn't in that class.

But Britny was. Probably she'd tell him what Catherine had done.

The bell rang, ending the class. Mrs. Olsen stopped reading. "We'll finish this tomorrow," she yelled above the commotion of kids getting up from their desks.

Catherine stood up. Several people were looking at her. Some were grinning. Britny Marsh sneered.

"Off in your dreams again, Catherine?" she muttered as she passed. "Get a life!"

Easy for her to say. Except for the cheerleader thing, Britny had everything a girl could want. She even had Travis Cavanaugh.

But not for long.

After the last period class, Catherine looked for Liz. They almost always walked home together. Liz lived with her aunt and uncle and their five kids just two blocks from where Catherine and her mother lived.

Today Liz was waiting as usual under the big oak in front of the school, but almost immediately she walked off ahead as Catherine approached.

Catherine caught up with her. "Is something wrong, Liz?"

"No, nothing's wrong." Liz turned her head to glance at Catherine, then looked ahead again. "My best friend is nutso over a dumb soap opera, and she talks to herself in class, but no, nothing's wrong."

Catherine stopped. "Are you embarrassed to walk with me, Liz? Because if you are, I can find my way home by myself."

Liz shifted her book bag from one shoulder to the other, then reached back and grabbed Catherine's arm. "Come on, dopey. Don't be so touchy."

Liz was taller and stronger, so Catherine couldn't keep from being drawn forward. For a moment they walked in silence. Then Catherine said, "Liz, tell me the truth. Do I really, honestly, truly look like Cassandra the way Travis said?"

"Yes, really, honestly, truly," Liz said. "If you cut your hair, you'd look just like her. Now forget the soap opera."

"What's the matter?" Catherine asked. "I thought you liked *Lost River* as much as I do."

"I like it! I like it!" Liz said. "But I don't obsess about it the way you do. I don't race over to Andersen's Appliances so I won't miss a single second of it. I don't go drifting off to fantasyland about Dr. Carlton Wyatt or some other dumb TV hunk while I'm supposed to be listening to dumb poetry that we'll be having a dumb test on next week."

"You don't talk to yourself either, do you, Liz?" Catherine could hear her voice rising.

Liz glanced around at passing students who looked their way.

"I'm embarrassing you, aren't I, Liz?" Catherine didn't seem to be able to stop the flow of words. "Well, *excuse me!* Maybe you'd like to write life scripts for me so I don't freak out my so-called friends."

She'd said too much. Overdramatized. She could tell by the look Liz gave her.

Still, she'd played the scene well. She'd sounded like Cassandra when she'd once mouthed off to Weston Fremont when he criticized her for the way she'd acted at a party.

Sometimes at home Catherine practiced saying things the way Cassandra did. She had kind of an accent, not British really, but precise and rounded.

Catherine realized she'd spaced out again when Liz gave a loud sigh, swung her book bag back to its original shoulder, and started walking rapidly toward home, leaving her behind.

So go, Liz. Who cared?

But this was Liz. They'd been best friends ever since Liz had moved to Greenville two years before.

Weren't friends supposed to stand by each other?

Slowly Catherine headed toward home. The camera was there again, recording her mournful face, her drooping walk.

It took her a long time to snail her way down the street past the football field and turn the corner to Jepsen Park.

It was there at the edge of the park that she saw it.

At first she didn't know what it was supposed to be. It was a Tide detergent box standing at the end of a small mound of dirt. On it was pasted a tombstone-shaped piece of paper with some writing on it.

Catherine moved closer to it so she could read the words, but suddenly her ankle twisted painfully and she fell to her knees. She hadn't seen the hole she'd stepped into, and she saw now that it had been partially covered over with grass.

Rubbing her ankle, she turned back to the

Tide box with the tombstone-shaped paper on it.

She could read the message now. *C.B.*, it said, and then on the next line, *Rest in peace.*

No. What it said was, *"C.B. Rest in pieces."*

C.B. Cassandra Bly.

Or . . . Catherine Belmont?

Catherine's heart hammered and she struggled to her feet. Her mouth was dry. Someone had put that ugly thing there for her!

She tried to run away, but her twisted ankle hurt.

She stopped, looking back at the thing.

Was somebody playing tricks on her? Was somebody giving her one more dig about being so addicted to a soap opera?

That had to be it. The soap box was the clue.

Somebody was probably at this very moment watching from some hidden spot, laughing about how clever the trick was.

She wasn't going to let that person know that she'd been frightened, even momentarily.

Trying to look casual despite her pounding heart and throbbing ankle, she kicked over the soap box, then, trying not to limp, she strolled on down the street as if nothing had happened.

But something *had* happened. Whoever had

set up that box had dug the hole for her to fall into.

Or maybe that was just the place where the person had scooped out the dirt to make the mound for the "grave." Maybe her injury had not been intentional.

She had to believe that. Who would want to hurt her?

She had gone not more than half a block when she heard a car coming.

Someone called her. "Hey, Cath!"

Kade's voice.

"Want a lift home?" he asked.

"Why not?" she said.

She climbed into his battered car and he gunned it off down the street.

"Were you limping?" Kade asked.

"No," she lied.

Kade could have been the one who had set up that soap box tombstone, just to tease her. Well, she wasn't going to give him the satisfaction of knowing that it had affected her in any way.

"What's up?" he asked. "Where's Liz? I thought you and her were like Siamese twins."

"You and she," Catherine corrected automatically.

"Whatever."

He sounded grumpy. She'd been correcting him since they were little kids, and she knew it drove him crazy.

"Did you and *she* . . ." he emphasized the word, " . . . have a blowup or something?"

"Yes," Catherine said shortly.

He waited.

Catherine signed. "Is it so weird to like a TV show a lot?"

"No," he said, "but. . . ."

"But what?"

He shook his head, keeping his eyes on the road. "But nothing. Forget it."

She knew he'd been going to rag her about being addicted to the soap opera. She sighed again. "If Mom would get our VCR fixed, I could tape the show at home and not embarrass my friends by running over to Andersen's Appliances at lunchtime."

"What's wrong with your VCR?"

"What's wrong is that we don't have the money to pay a repair bill." She looked up ahead to see where Liz had gone but didn't see her. "What's wrong is that Mom thinks it's more important to buy bread and veggies than to get our VCR fixed."

"I'll take a look at it," Kade said. "Maybe I can fix it."

That surprised her. These days it always

surprised her when Kade stopped teasing and was nice.

Biting back a smart remark, she said simply, "I'd appreciate that, Kade."

He turned into the driveway between their two houses. Or rather, between his parents' house and Old Albert Baxter's house where Catherine and her mother rented an apartment on the second floor.

Out of the corner of her eye she saw a curtain twitch and knew Old Albert was watching from his downstairs living room. Old Albert watched everything. If she so much as dropped a gum wrapper in his driveway, he was there yelling at her to pick it up. Fussy Old Albert.

Kade stopped the car. "I'll come up and get the VCR right now."

"Okay." Catherine got out and led the way up the outside stairway to the little balcony which sported a flourishing potted ficus tree. She was sure Old Albert was watching and listening. He'd probably come charging out in a minute to yell that Kade couldn't go up there when her mother wasn't home.

Her mother was never home on weekday afternoons. She was the late shift cafeteria manager at a factory that ran full blast around the clock.

Catherine opened the screen door, then unlocked the front door and motioned for Kade to follow her inside.

Late afternoon sunlight splashed through the large windows and lit up the living room with its beige shag rug.

Dumping her books on the little table inside the front door, Catherine went to the TV, which sat next to the big double window facing Kade's house.

"Here it is." She pulled the VCR from a shelf under the TV, checking to see that there was a tape inside.

"The tape's the one I record *Lost River* on," she said. "You can use it if you need to."

"Okay," Kade said. He picked up the machine. "Might be just a loose connection or something. I'll let you know." He stood there looking at her.

Maybe she should offer him a Pepsi or something. But she didn't really want him to stay. She wanted to be alone so she could think about Cassandra and Dr. Carlton Wyatt and how he'd saved her life and how they were going to fall in love.

She wanted to soak her twisted ankle.

She wanted to think about Travis Cavanaugh.

She held the door open for Kade, and he left without another word.

Catherine examined her ankle, but it wasn't swollen. It was beginning to feel better, so instead of soaking it she made herself a peanut butter sandwich, then turned on the TV and lay down on the sofa, pulling the old blue afghan over her. She was tired. Munching contentedly, she watched the end of *The Oprah Winfrey Show*.

She didn't mean to fall asleep, but she did. She dreamed of Dr. Carlton Wyatt, who held a gleaming scalpel in his hand as he came toward her. The scalpel dripped blood, and Dr. Wyatt's eyes glittered as he came closer, step by step.

No, it wasn't Dr. Carlton Wyatt at all. It was Travis Cavanaugh, and in his hand he held a single red rose, dripping blood.

Catherine awoke suddenly, as if an alarm had gone off. She'd heard a noise. She didn't know whether it had been inside the apartment or on the little balcony outside.

She sat up quickly, and that's when she saw it.

On the small table beside the sofa was a slender white vase holding a single red rose.

A *blood*red rose.

Chapter 3

Catherine leaped off the sofa, screaming. There was a slight twinge in her ankle, but she ignored it.

Somebody had been there. Somebody had come into the apartment while she slept and left the rose on the little table. A bloodred rose, just like the one somebody had placed on Cassandra's chest after the accident, and the one left next to her hospital bed.

Catherine's skin crawled. She stopped screaming, but she felt stiff and cold as she stared at the rose in its white vase.

What did it mean?

Who had been there?

Trying to calm herself, she walked over to check the outside door. It was unlocked. She remembered she hadn't locked it after Kade left. But that wasn't unusual. There wasn't a whole lot of crime in Greenville and she and her mother almost always left the door unlocked.

Maybe she should go outside and yell for Kade.

Kade.

Her pulse slowed.

Kade had left the rose. She was sure of it. This was just more of his teasing, like the soapbox tombstone.

He'd left this rose as a joke. It was the kind of thing he'd think was funny.

Still, she wished he hadn't come into the apartment like that. It gave her the creeps to think of him standing there looking down at her while she slept.

Picking up the rose, she carried it outside to the little balcony. If Kade thought this was a big joke, she'd go along with it.

"Kade," she yelled. He'd hear her if he was in his room.

He was. He stuck his head out of his window. "Whaddya want? I'm watching a *Star Trek* rerun."

"How come you're not working on my VCR?"

"Gimme a break," he said. "I have to psych myself up to it."

She gave him a big smile, then stuck the rose in her teeth, flung her arms in the air, tossed her head. Careful not to make her ankle hurt too much, she stamped her feet like a flamenco dancer.

Cassandra had put on an act like this once when Weston Fremont had given her a rose.

Taking the rose from her teeth Catherine looked over at Kade. "Just wanted to say thanks," she said, her words precise and rounded, like Cassandra's.

Kade bugged his eyes and put a leg over his windowsill as if he were going to crawl out. "Wow," he hollered. "How about saying it again?"

She repeated her performance, then stuck out her tongue, tossed the rose over the railway of the balcony, leaning over to see where it landed.

Suddenly the railing gave way. If Catherine hadn't caught a solid post, she would have plunged to the concrete driveway below.

"Hey," Kade yelled. "That wasn't part of the act, was it?" His face was concerned.

"No," she said as soon as she could speak. How could he even consider that she'd spatter her brains on the cement below as "part of the act"?

Somebody must have loosened the railing. Somebody who knew she leaned against it every now and then. Somebody who knew just *where* she leaned against it.

Shakily she backed up until she felt the solid wall behind her.

She could have been killed!

"It's needed repairing for a long time," Kade said calmly. "I guess it just worked itself loose. Want me to come fix it?"

Maybe he already *had* fixed it. She couldn't believe he'd do something like that, though. Not Kade. He was a joker, but he wouldn't want to see her hurt. Would he?

"No." She shook her head hard. "You fix my VCR. I'll tell Old Albert about this." She didn't want Kade coming over.

She hoped Old Albert hadn't heard what she said. She always called him Mr. Baxter to his face. He'd hate her more than ever if he'd heard her being disrespectful.

Maybe *he'd* messed up the railing.

No, not Old Albert. He hated everybody. She hardly thought he'd concentrate just on her.

Maybe the railing had worked itself loose, the way Kade said.

She went downstairs to ask Old Albert politely if he'd do the repair work.

* * *

Usually Liz came by each morning and waited downstairs for Catherine to walk with her, but the next morning she wasn't there.

Kade was, however. He waved to her from his car.

"Want to ride to school with me and your VCR?" he asked, reaching over to open the passenger door.

She climbed in. The VCR sat in the back with a seat belt around it. "Why are you taking my VCR to school?"

"I think I found what's wrong," he said. "I'm taking it to my electronics class. I'll check it out on the equipment there."

"Okay," she said. "Think it's something you can fix?"

Kade backed the car out of the driveway. "If I can't, maybe Travis can. He's pretty good at stuff like that."

Travis. The day was suddenly brighter, the way it had been yesterday after she'd met Travis.

"Is he in your electronics class?" she asked casually as if she didn't care one way or another.

"Yes." The tires squealed going around a corner. It was always an adventure riding with Kade. "I told you yesterday he was in one of my classes," he said, then added, "Britny's in the class, too. Maybe I should get *her* to fix it."

It figured. Britny was smart, along with everything else. She took advanced physics and chemistry. And electronics. So why did she get so angry when Catherine won the cheerleading position?

"Did Old Albert fix your railing?" Kade asked.

"Yes," she said.

"Lucky thing you didn't get hurt when that thing gave way." Suddenly Kade braked to a stop and honked. "There's Liz. Think she wants a ride?"

"I don't know." Catherine wondered if Liz would get in the same car with her after their fight yesterday.

But Liz came running over, threw her book bag onto the backseat, and climbed in beside it. "Thanks, Kade," she said. "Hi, Cath."

Apparently she hadn't been nursing any hard feelings. "Hi," Catherine said. "You weren't at my house so I thought you weren't coming."

"No problem." Liz settled in beside the VCR. "I was running late. I had to help get the little kids ready for school. My aunt's not feeling well."

"I'm sorry," Catherine said.

Lots of times Liz had to take care of her

young cousins. Sometimes she told Catherine how much she envied her, living alone with just her mother. Liz's own mother had been sick for a long time in another town, which was why she didn't live with her. Catherine had never met her. Liz said her father had skipped years before, and she hardly ever mentioned him.

In the backseat, Liz was examining the VCR and commenting on the seat belt that held it firmly in place. She and Kade launched into a discussion of the many uses of seat belts, including their ability to hold small cousins firmly in one spot.

"They like to play 'going someplace,'" Liz said. "I strap them into my aunt's car and I just sit and read while they pretend we're driving down the freeway."

Kade laughed and said something about kids.

The talk about seat belts reminded Catherine of how Cassandra's belt had broken and allowed her to be thrown from her little convertible when it went off the road. She remembered how the camera had zoomed in on the belt dangling from the overturned car. Somebody had cut it, just as somebody had done something to the steering and brakes.

She didn't want to miss today's show, but

there was a noon cheerleading practice. How was she going to work that out?

She didn't tune in to Liz and Kade again until they got to the parking lot at school.

"I'll probably get it fixed this morning," Kade said as he unbuckled the belt from around the VCR. "I'll tape your soap opera for you, Cath, so you don't have to break the speed limit getting to Andersen's. Nobody will be in the classroom at noon, so I'll just hook it up to the TV we've got there and let it run. I'll make an extra on another machine just in case this one doesn't work right."

"Great." Catherine was glad she didn't have to choose between the show and cheerleading practice. If she missed practice more than once, they'd give the job to somebody else.

Probably Britny.

"By the way," Kade said, grinning at her. "That was some show you put on for me last night."

Liz looked interested. "Show? What show?"

Catherine grinned back at Kade. She was feeling good all of a sudden. "Since you were kind enough to leave me a rose, I thought I should make use of it."

Kade looked puzzled. "What rose?"

"What rose do you think, dummy? The one

I had in my teeth. The one you left on the table by my bed."

In your *teeth*?" Liz sounded bewildered.

Kade was shaking his head. "I didn't leave any rose," he said. "You're really slipping right into that soap opera, Cath."

Picking up the VCR, he walked away.

"Kade," Catherine called. "Wait." She hurried to catch up with him. "Kade, did you leave something in Jepsen Park yesterday for me to find?"

He put on such a genuinely puzzled look that she couldn't be sure anymore that he'd done it. He wasn't that good an actor, was he?

"Forget it." She felt cold. Who else would have done it?

She told Liz about the tombstone and the rose as they hurried to class. Was Kade really totally innocent, she wondered aloud.

"Has he ever given you roses?" Liz asked.

"He's never given me anything except chicken pox," Catherine said.

But who else except Kade would come right inside her house? And certainly he could have left the soap box tombstone and still have had time to drive around the park and pick her up, the day before.

But anyone could have set up the soap box.

And anyone who came up on the little balcony at her home could have looked through the leaves of the ficus tree into the window and seen her asleep on the sofa. Anyone could have sneaked in without waking her. Anyone could have loosened the balcony railing.

"It wasn't you, was it, Liz?" Catherine asked.

"I'll pretend you didn't say that," Liz said. "I think Kade's right. You're really beginning to live in that soap opera."

Did it again, Catherine thought, as Liz stomped off ahead of her. Mentally she shook herself. Was she getting paranoid or what? These were her best friends that she was suspecting.

"Wait for me," she called to Liz. "I apologize."

But if her best friends hadn't left the rose and the tombstone, then who had?

The cheerleading practice at noon was a disaster as far as Catherine was concerned. They were out on the football field where the marching band was rehearsing. Britny was in the band, and Catherine knew she was watching the cheerleaders. But when Catherine whirled once and caught Britny staring right at her, she merely blew a practice scale on her clarinet and looked the other way.

Could Britny have left the rose? Had *she* set up the soap box tombstone and dug the little pit in front so Catherine would twist her ankle? Was she willing to do that much to get the cheerleading job?

But certainly she hadn't broken the balcony railing.

Had she?

Catherine hadn't added up all the things that had happened before, but now, suddenly, it seemed as if somebody was after her just as surely as somebody was after Cassandra. Somebody who meant to do her fearful harm.

She was so unraveled by her thoughts that she tripped over her own feet. She thought that Mrs. Riveros, the cheerleading advisor, would surely kick her off the squad, but instead Mrs. Riveros chose her as one of three girls to do a routine for a coming assembly.

"Suzanne, Erin, and Catherine," Mrs. Riveros said. "Sign up for the auditorium after school tomorrow so you can practice on the stage." She looked straight at Catherine. "And I do mean *practice*, Belmont."

It sounded like a warning.

But one good thing happened that day. Kade got her VCR fixed and taped *Lost River* for her.

He gave her and Liz a ride home, dropping Liz off first. When they got to Catherine's house, Kade carried the VCR upstairs as Old Albert watched from his kitchen window.

"I hope it's going to work all right," Kade said as he hooked it up to the TV.

She knew he was hinting to stay and watch the show with her, but she didn't invite him. She wanted to be alone. She'd get a snack from the fridge and stretch out on the sofa with the comforting old blue afghan over her while she watched. She didn't feel like listening to Kade's smart-mouth remarks about the show.

"It'll be fine," she said. "Thanks, Kade."

He turned on the TV and VCR. "I rewound your tape back to the beginning," he said, pushing the play button.

"Thanks." Catherine sat down as the familiar theme music played and the show began.

Cassandra, pale and groggy, lay in her hospital bed. Her head was no longer bandaged, and her short hair looked dark against the white pillow. A starched nurse hovered over her.

Kade shuffled his feet. "Okay. It works." He took a couple of steps toward the door.

Catherine didn't say anything.

Okay," he said again. "Let me know if you need me again."

Catherine got up and locked both the screen door and the door after he left. She wasn't going to take any more chances on having somebody come into the apartment.

She hurried back to look at the TV screen.

Cassandra was staring at the rose on the white table beside her bed.

"Who left that rose?" she asked the nurse.

"I don't know, dear," the nurse said. "It must have been somebody here in the hospital. Nobody else is allowed in this area."

Cassandra smiled. "It must have been Dr. Wyatt," she said.

Just then the door swung open and Dr. Wyatt came in. He still wore his green surgical suit and cap. His stethoscope dangled from around his neck.

"Did I hear my name?" he asked, smiling at Cassandra.

Cassandra's eyes were luminous. "It wasn't enough that you saved my life," she said softly, "but you gave me a rose, too."

Dr. Wyatt looked at the rose. "I didn't give you that." His eyes darkened, and Catherine knew he was remembering that other bloodred rose, the one that had been lying across Cassandra's body when she was brought in.

Suddenly the picture faded out. There were some blips and wavy lines, and another scene came on.

For a moment Catherine thought it was a commercial. There was a scene in a park. The girl in the scene looked very familiar. Cassandra?

With a start, Catherine realized it was herself. Somebody had videotaped her.

It had been done yesterday when she'd found the soap box tombstone. It showed her stumbling into the hole and sprawling on the ground. There was a close-up of her face as she felt the pain of the twisted ankle. The camera stayed focused on her face, showing her fright as she read the initials and words written on the fake tombstone.

It backed off then, to show her struggling to her feet and trying to run. She'd stopped, peering around as if to see who might be watching. Her eyes had narrowed. That had been when she'd realized that somebody must be playing a trick on her.

After she kicked over the box and limped away, the camera zoomed in on the epitaph,

C.B.
REST IN PIECES.

There were some more blips on the screen, then the camera swung around to focus on a crudely printed sign which said,

ENJOY YOUR SOAP OPERA LIFE
WHILE YOU CAN, C.B.

Chapter 4

Catherine felt ill. Her hands were clammy and her head pounded.

Was she actually slipping into the soap opera the way Kade said?

Quickly she rewound the tape back to the start of the scene where she appeared. She played it again.

This was impossible. How could there be a scene with her in it right in the middle of the *Lost River* episode?

Weakly she leaned back against the sofa cushions, trying to pull together her shattered thoughts. Think, she told herself. Try to make some sense out of this.

It *was* possible, of course. Somebody with a camcorder had apparently shot the scene of her and the soap box tombstone, then edited it into the recorded tape.

But who could it be? Kade was the obvious

choice. Kade could have used the camcorder from his electronics class to shoot the scene in the park the day before. He'd had full access to her VCR today and could have done anything he wanted to with the tape in it.

But lots of people had camcorders. And other people had had access to the VCR. Catherine's mind replayed Kade's voice telling her that Travis was in his electronics class. And Britny.

But Travis had no reason to play tricks on her. He didn't even know her, except as the girl in Andersen's Appliances shop.

And Britny? She'd been out on the football field with the marching band during the time the show had been taped. When could she have done the editing?

It *must* have been Kade. He could have set up the tombstone scene yesterday. He'd probably planned to sneak the tape into her apartment the way he'd sneaked the rose in, but then a perfect opportunity had presented itself when she'd asked him to fix the VCR.

But she hadn't asked him. He'd *volunteered* to fix the VCR. Probably he'd been chuckling to himself all the time about what he was going to do.

Running to the door, she opened it and stepped out onto the little balcony. "KADE," she roared. "You slime. Come out and talk to me!"

This time he didn't pop his head out of his window.

"KADE," she yelled again. "Answer me, you rat!"

From downstairs, Old Albert whammed the ceiling with his broom handle. "Quiet," he bellowed.

"Stifle," she whispered to herself, then hurried down the stairs, letting her heels clatter with each step. Old Albert was such a pain.

Crossing the lawn from her house to Kade's, she hurried up the porch steps and battered her fists against his door. "KADE," she shouted.

No answer.

His parents and sister wouldn't be home from work yet, and very likely Kade had taken off, knowing how angry she'd be over this latest trick he'd pulled.

"KADE!" she yelled once more. "You creep!"

She walked back to look down the driveway, checking to see if his car was there.

It wasn't.

"I'll wait," she said aloud, plopping herself down on the top porch step.

She sat there for several minutes before she

realized how silly it was. Kade could hang out somewhere for hours, just to avoid her.

Catherine stood up and headed back to her own home, suppressing an impulse to look over her shoulder to see if anyone was following her.

The apartment seemed empty and hollow when she got inside. She went immediately to the big window and pulled the drapes. Somebody could be watching from outside.

Too nervous to study, she paced back and forth across the room for several minutes, trying to think. The only thing that was clear was that she didn't want to be there alone.

Hurrying to the telephone, she punched in Liz's number.

"Come over," she said when Liz answered.

Liz must have heard the terror in her voice because she said simply, "I'm there."

While she waited, Catherine rewound the VCR tape to where *Lost River* started. She wouldn't tell Liz ahead of time about the scene that had been spliced in. She'd just let it be a surprise. That would jump-start Liz's mind, and together they'd decide what to do about Kade.

It wasn't long before she heard Liz running up the stairs. Old Albert heard her, too. His broom handle whumped against his ceiling and his quavery voice yelled out something that Catherine couldn't hear.

"What's up?" Liz panted when Catherine opened the door.

"I want you to watch something with me," Catherine said. "Sit down." She pointed to the sofa.

Liz sat, and Catherine sat beside her. She turned on the VCR.

Once again the familiar theme music played, and once again Cassandra gazed luminously at Dr. Wyatt as she thanked him for the rose. Once again he said he hadn't given it to her, and his eyes darkened as he remembered the other rose, the one that had been on her body when the ambulance brought her in.

"Now," Catherine said. "Watch this."

The scene faded, and there was a commercial about a nauseous stomach being soothed by an antacid liquid. Catherine didn't remember seeing it the first time she'd played the tape.

The next scene started.

Detective Doug Haskell of the Lost River Police Department inspected Cassandra's wrecked car. Examining the severed seat belt, he said, "I think we have a case of attempted homicide here."

"Wait," Catherine said. "That scene wasn't there before."

Snatching up the hand control, she backed up the tape to where Dr. Wyatt said again that he hadn't given Cassandra the rose. Then came the commercial and the scene with the wrecked car. Again Detective Haskell suspected attempted homicide.

"Something's wrong." Catherine punched the rewind button again. Once again Dr. Wyatt declared he hadn't given Cassandra the rose, and once again the commercial came on. Once again Detective Haskell fingered the broken seat belt.

No blips. No black screen. No edited segment of Catherine and the soap box tombstone.

"I'll bite," Liz said. "What is there about that commercial that you find so fascinating?"

"Liz." Catherine could hear how tight her own voice sounded. "There was something else on the tape. *I* was on the tape. There was a scene of me seeing that soap box yesterday."

"What?" Liz sounded astonished.

"I mean it. Somebody videotaped me there in the park."

Liz grinned slyly as if waiting for Catherine to tell her the punch line.

"No, really," Catherine said, poking the rewind button once again. "It was there. The whole scene I told you about, with the tombstone and the fake grave. It showed me looking at it, then the camera went in for a close-up of the tombstone with the words about 'Rest in pieces.' After that, it shifted to a sign that said, 'Enjoy your soap opera life while you can, C.B.'"

Liz was quiet for a moment, then she reached out to feel Catherine's forehead. "Cath, sweetie, does your head hurt or something? I mean, you've been watching a lot of this show lately. Maybe . . ."

Catherine pushed away her hand. "I'm not sick, Liz. And I'm not crazy. It *happened*."

"Oka-a-a-a-y." Liz drew out the word. "So where is it now?"

"Kade came and changed tapes, Liz. I'm sure of it." She told about going over to his house to yell at him. "I didn't lock the door, and while I was gone he must have come in and changed tapes. That *has* to be what happened."

"Oka-a-a-y," Liz said again.

Catherine could tell she didn't believe her.

Liz looked at the TV screen where Cassandra was still lying in her hospital bed. "So what do you want to do about it, Cath?"

"I'd like to get even with Kade."

Liz nodded. "How?"

"I don't know," Catherine said. "Maybe we could set up a scene to scare *him*."

"How?" Liz asked again, sounding concerned.

Catherine went to the kitchen and brought back a scissors. "First of all, I want you to cut my hair."

"Oh Cath, no." Liz was clearly distressed. "Your long hair is so pretty. Why do you want to cut it?"

"I've been thinking about doing it anyway," Catherine told her calmly. "And right now I want to look as much like Cassandra as possible."

Liz's eyes widened. "Cath, you're getting too into that soap opera."

Catherine held the scissors out to Liz. "Do it."

Liz backed away.

"Look," Catherine said patiently, "I'm not slipping over the edge. Really. I'm fine. It's just that I want to make Kade *think* that's what has happened. I want him to think he's responsible."

She could tell Liz was weakening.

"We could really give Kade a scare," she wheedled. "He deserves it for doing all those things to me. And to tell the truth, I've been planning to go have my hair cut anyway. So save me the beauty parlor price and I'll take you out for a burger."

"Well." Liz reached for the scissors. "Cath, I'm doing this under protest. I guess you're determined to ruin yourself." Suddenly she grinned. "But I can't wait to see Kade's face when he thinks he's really sent you over."

Liz was a genius with a scissors, even a dull pair like Catherine's mother's kitchen shears. She'd had lots of practice cutting the hair of her little cousins.

She rewound the VCR to a scene with Cassandra. Looking closely at the TV screen, she snipped and styled Catherine's hair.

When she was finished, she escorted Catherine over to the big mirror that hung on the west wall across from the front door.

"Look," she said.

Catherine looked. She would have sworn she was seeing Cassandra.

Suddenly she had a few misgivings. Not that she didn't like the cut, because she did. But she looked so very much like Cassandra that it was scary.

It was as if she truly *was* Cassandra.

"It's great," Liz said. "You were pretty with long hair, but you're spectacular this way.

Travis Cavanaugh is going to flip, if that's what you want."

Catherine was embarrassed. What was Travis going to think when she showed up as Cassandra's twin right after he'd told her they looked alike? Would he think she'd done it to please him? She hadn't thought of that.

"I should have brought our camcorder," Liz said, stepping back to admire Catherine. "I'd like to record this event."

That's right. Liz's aunt did have a camcorder. They took lots of pictures of the kids.

Liz could have taped the segment of Catherine looking at the soap box tombstone.

But she didn't have the camcorder with her yesterday, did she?

Or did she? It might have been in her book bag.

Catherine was ashamed of her own thoughts. It was almost a relief to hear footsteps on the stairs outside.

"Must be Dr. Carlton Wyatt," Liz whispered, grinning.

Catherine peeked out of the window. "It's Kade." She glanced quickly around the room. "Liz," she said, "back up the tape to that scene where Cassandra is in the hospital bed."

Quickly Liz rewound the tape. Catherine lay down on the sofa, pulling the blue afghan up over her body. She tried to look pale and weak.

Liz opened the door for Kade. "I'm glad you're here," she whispered. "Something terrible has happened to Catherine."

"What's wrong with her?" Kade sounded alarmed.

"I don't know," Liz whispered. "It's really spooky. I think she's actually becoming Cassandra. Come look."

She led a bewildered-looking Kade over to the sofa where Catherine lay. "See for yourself," she told him.

Through half-closed eyes Catherine saw Kade bend over her. Behind him, on the TV screen, she could see Dr. Carlton Wyatt leaning over Cassandra's bed. It gave her an odd feeling to be duplicating the scene on the TV.

"She's cut her hair," Kade whispered. "Like Cassandra's."

Liz nodded, pointing at the TV screen.

Kade turned to look at Cassandra, then back at Catherine. "This is weird," he said. "She's really flipping out. Do you think we should call a doctor?"

"No," Liz whispered. "Let's wait. Maybe we can bring her out of it." She came close to Catherine and suddenly clapped her hands.

It took every ounce of control Catherine had not to blink.

"No response," Liz muttered. "Come out to the kitchen, Kade, where we can talk."

They tiptoed from the room. Catherine sat up. Kade must be scared enough now to admit he'd set this whole thing up. He must be feeling really guilty by now.

She was ready to call out, to tell Kade it was a joke just like the ones he'd been playing, but just then the telephone rang.

As she reached out to pick it up, there was another ring. This one was from the TV. The telephone by Cassandra's bed.

"Hello," Catherine said, just as Cassandra said it, a mere second out of synch.

At first she could barely hear the voice in her ear. It was muffled and strange, as if the speaker had something over his — or her — mouth.

Then more clearly it said, "How did you like the red rose, C.B.? The bloody red rose?"

Catherine slammed the telephone down at the same moment that Cassandra did.

Her heart pounded. The words on Cassandra's phone were the exact ones she'd heard in her own ear, delayed the length of a breath. *How did you like the red rose, C.B.? The bloody red rose?*

Chapter 5

"Liz!" Catherine screamed. "Kade! Come here."

Her throat was so tight she could scarcely get the words out. Had they even heard her?

"Liz!" She was sobbing now and could barely speak.

Nobody came. Had Liz and Kade gone, leaving her alone?

The TV was still on. Someone was screaming on the screen. Or was it coming from her own throat?

Catherine slid off the sofa and staggered toward the kitchen door. "Liz," she whispered hopelessly.

Behind her, from the TV, came Cassandra's voice. *"Who is doing this to me?" she said. "Who is trying to kill me?"*

Catherine pushed against the swinging door to the kitchen and almost fell when it swung open. "Who is trying to kill me?" she gasped.

Kade and Liz stared at her in alarm. Kade, who'd been leaning against the refrigerator, leaped toward her, grabbing her arm and guiding her to a kitchen chair where she sat down.

"Kill you?" he said. "What do you mean, Cath?"

Liz came over to kneel at her side. Gazing into her face, she said, "Cath. Tell us what happened."

Catherine lifted an arm, gone suddenly heavy, to point toward the living room where the TV still babbled. "Cassandra," she said. "No, not Cassandra. Me. There was a phone call."

"On the show?" Liz asked. "A phone call? What was it about?"

"No. Not on the show." She shook her head in confusion. "Yes, on the show, too. But someone called *me*."

Liz looked up at Kade. "Did you hear the phone ring?"

"I heard *a* phone ring," Kade said. "I thought it was on the TV."

Catherine tried to stop the trembling of her hands by clasping them together. "It was. But my phone rang, too. And the person whispered the exact same words someone was saying to Cassandra on the show."

Liz looked up at Kade again, then back at Catherine. "What words, Cath?"

Catherine swallowed. "The person said, 'How did you like the red rose, C.B.? The bloody red rose.' That's what somebody said to Cassandra, too."

"The very same words?" Kade asked.

Catherine nodded. "The very same words at almost the very same time."

"*Almost?*"

Catherine tried to control her voice. "There was a slight delay. Almost like an echo."

Liz looked at her thoughtfully, then tried a small smile. "Okay, Cath, what's the joke? Are you trying to spook us or something, because that sure is what you're doing. Are you still trying to get back at Kade?"

Kade looked bewildered. "Back at me? For what?"

"I was sure you pulled that whole tombstone thing and all the rest," Catherine told him. "But you *didn't* because you're *here*." She knew she wasn't making sense, but she couldn't put her thoughts together to explain.

She shook her head hard, trying to clear it. "I'm telling the truth, Liz. I'm telling you that I heard the same words come over my phone at the same time that Cassandra heard them."

Liz's look changed to one of concern. "Cath,

you really are into this thing too far. Maybe you'd better stop watching the show for a while." She reached out to touch Catherine's hair. "The haircut is what did it. I'm sorry I let you talk me into doing it."

"What do you mean?" Catherine asked.

Liz picked up one of Catherine's hands and began rubbing it gently. "Well, see, it's like Kade says. You've been slipping into that soap opera for a long time. Pretending to be Cassandra, I mean. Dressing like her. Talking like her. Then after Travis said you *look* like her, you wanted your hair cut like hers. You *became* her. You just had a little lapse of reality, Cath. You'll be okay."

Catherine's heart began to pound again. Whose side was Liz on? "It *happened*, Liz. Don't you believe me?"

"I'd like to," Liz said. "But what you're telling us is impossible."

Kade hadn't said anything for a while. Now he spoke. "Well, it's *possible*. But not very probable." He headed back into the living room. "Let's go take a look around."

Catherine's legs were weak, but with Liz's help she stood up and followed him. "What are we looking for?"

"An explanation," Kade said. "A bug."

"Bug?" Catherine's mind sluggishly explored the word as Liz helped her to the sofa.

Kade, busy running his fingers around the TV, the VCR, and the cabinet they sat on, nodded. "Somebody *could* have planted an electronic listening device somewhere." He said it as if he thought it was pretty farfetched. "They *could* be listening in to what's going on here, and they *could* have called at the same time as the call came through to Cassandra."

Catherine's breath caught in a small, left-over sob. "But how could they say the same words?"

"The show was taped," Kade said gently. "Anybody who saw it earlier would know what was coming next."

Liz picked up the telephone, felt all around it, and put it down. "There's nothing on this."

Catherine took a deep, shaky breath. "You mean there might be a logical explanation for that phone call?"

Kade hesitated for just a moment, then said, "Let's just say that a little electronic magic *could* explain everything." He got down to feel around the bottom of the sofa.

"Not everything," Catherine said. "A bug could explain the how. But how about the *why?*"

Liz and Kade looked at each other.

Then Liz said, "Cath, no one would want to

hurt you. Are you *absolutely* sure there was a call? Are you *absolutely* sure you weren't being Cassandra at that moment?"

"No," Catherine said miserably. "I'm not sure of anything anymore." They hadn't believed a word she'd said.

They didn't find a bug. So maybe what Liz and Kade suspected was true. Catherine had become so obsessed with the show that she'd slid into Cassandra's character. She'd wanted to *be* Cassandra, with Dr. Carlton Wyatt adoring her as he healed her injuries.

She had no proof that there had ever been a soap box tombstone. She should have picked it up, should have taken it with her, should have shown it to somebody else.

"I watched myself on the show," she whispered.

"What do you mean, watched yourself?" Kade sounded totally bewildered.

Catherine explained about the segment on the tape the day before. She told about the soap box tombstone and how somebody had taped the scene and edited it into today's tape.

"Why didn't you yell for me?" Kade said. "I would have come."

"I did yell." Catherine felt tired. She wanted all this to be over. "You weren't home."

"Okay, then," Kade said, "let's see the tape."

"It's gone." That edited tape was another thing she should have saved. She should have taken it out of the VCR right after she'd played it.

"Gone? Cath . . . don't you think you could be mistaken?"

She was too tired to explain. "Kade," she said slowly, "who knew it was my VCR that you had in your electronics classroom?"

Suddenly she had a flash of him telling everybody that it was hers, and saying what a soap opera watcher she was and how they should give her a little jolt to scare her out of it. Such a good way to get even with her for laughing when he'd asked for a date.

"I didn't tell *anybody* it was yours," Kade said. "And everybody was gone to lunch while it was taping." He pinched his lower lip. "Maybe we should think about why you are so. . . ."

He paused. Catherine knew he'd been about to say "obsessed," or maybe "paranoid," but he changed it.

"Who knows that you always watch the show?" Kade finished.

The whole school knew she watched the

show. The kids, the teachers, the principal, the school nurse, the custodians, the bus drivers. Who *didn't* know?

Her face burned as she realized how foolish she must look to everybody. How foolish she was to sink into the show, to let herself become Cassandra.

Taking a deep breath, she said, "Thanks, you guys. I won't keep you any longer. I'm okay now. I guess my imagination got away from me."

They both looked relieved, happy that she'd at last come to her senses.

"Want me to stay until your mother comes home?" Liz asked.

"No." Catherine would have been glad to have her stay, but she wanted them to know she was all right. "I'll be fine, Liz. Thanks. I wish you'd both come over after school tomorrow, though. I'll tape the show again and we can watch it together."

Both Liz and Kade said they'd come.

"And," Catherine said, "if I need help tonight, I'll yell for Kade."

Kade nodded, his face serious. "I'll be there."

Catherine couldn't help but think that he just might be there, all right, listening through some kind of electronic thing. He seemed to know so much about them.

Then she was ashamed again for thinking such a thing.

After Liz and Kade left, Catherine sat at the kitchen table trying to do her homework. But her mind kept sliding back to the taped scene starring her, the loose balcony railing, the phone call. The bloodred rose.

Things had started happening right after she met Travis. His statement about how much she looked like Cassandra could very well have triggered something that made her think she *was* Cassandra.

The rose had certainly been real. So had the soap box tombstone. But her first thoughts had been that somebody was teasing her, and she'd probably been right. And the balcony railing — well, that had needed fixing for a long time.

She decided not to tell her mother about any of it. She was always so tired when she came home, and certainly didn't need any more worries laid on her. She'd been having personnel problems at the cafeteria and sometimes had to fill in on various jobs when people left unexpectedly.

But when Mom got home she wasn't so tired that she didn't notice Catherine's haircut right away.

"It's pretty," she said. "You remind me of somebody."

"Cassandra Bly," Catherine said. "On *Lost River*."

"Bingo." Her mother admired her from all angles. "Well, I must say it's very becoming. Maybe I should start calling you Cassandra."

"Catherine will do," Catherine said quickly. "Mom, can I fix you a snack?"

Her mom shook her head. "I ate at the cafeteria. I'm just going to take a hot bath and go to bed." She headed for her room. Looking back over her shoulder she said, "How's everything at school these days?"

"Fine." Then, hardly realizing she was going to say it, she said, "I met a new guy. His name is Travis. Travis Cavanaugh. I feel as if I've known him somewhere before. Mom, do you know any Cavanaughs?"

Her mother stopped short. For the length of a breath she stood there, her back stiff. Then she turned. "No." Her voice was tight and strained. "I don't." She put a hand to her forehead. "I used to know a Travis, but I don't think I've ever known any Cavanaughs."

Turning again, she walked quickly into her bedroom and closed the door.

Catherine started after her. What had made her hesitate?

At the bedroom door Catherine stopped. She knew from past experience that when her mother clammed up, she stayed clammed.

But something had clearly frightened her.

Or was that, too, just Catherine's overactive imagination?

She was so far into her thoughts that she nearly leapt through the ceiling when the telephone rang.

"I'll get it," she called to her mother. But her hand shook as she reached for it and brought it to her ear.

"Hello?" she said.

"Hello?" said the deep voice on the phone. "Hello? This is Dr. Carlton Wyatt."

Chapter 6

Catherine slammed down the telephone.

She couldn't breathe. What was happening? Why was Dr. Carlton Wyatt calling *her*? Wasn't he with Cassandra?

She wanted to cry out, but terror strangled her, choking off the scream before it could form.

Dr. Carlton Wyatt *couldn't* have called her. Dr. Carlton Wyatt was not even a real person. He was just a character on a soap opera. How, then, had she heard his voice on her telephone?

There was only one explanation. She had slipped so far into the soap opera that she no longer knew reality from fantasy.

She collapsed on the sofa, trying to get control of herself.

"Think, Catherine," she said aloud. "Don't just react."

That was something Mrs. Stewart was always saying in psych class. It hadn't meant much to Catherine before this.

She concentrated on drawing a couple of deep, shaky breaths.

"Now," she said aloud, "look at this calmly."

She was talking to herself, like Old Albert sometimes did. She was totally losing her grip. She hoped her mother hadn't heard her.

The telephone squatted silently there on its small table beside the sofa. She hardly dared look at it for fear it would ring again. Or she would *imagine* that it rang again.

Catherine thought back to the other phone call, the one where somebody had said the same words that were being said on the TV screen. The ring had been just a beat ahead of the ring of the TV phone. Each word had been completed before the same word was echoed on the show.

That call had been real. It *had* happened.

She *had* heard Dr. Carlton Wyatt's voice.

Something prodded at her mind. She'd been so frightened by that call that she hadn't really heard what went on right after it. Hadn't Dr. Wyatt snatched the telephone away from Cassandra? What had he said?

With a trembling hand, Catherine turned on the TV and reached for the VCR control. She backed the tape up to the phone call scene.

Cassandra picked up the telephone. A voice said, "How did you like the rose, C.B., the bloody red rose?"

Looking terrified, Cassandra dropped the phone.

"What's the matter?" Dr. Wyatt demanded.

Cassandra fell back against her pillows, her eyes wild and staring.

Dr. Wyatt snatched the handpiece she'd dropped. "Hello?" he said. "Hello? This is Dr. Carlton Wyatt."

That was the voice Catherine had heard on her phone. Those were the words.

So somebody could have played them from a tape of the show directly into the phone. Electronic magic, Kade had called it.

Knowing that it could have happened didn't calm Catherine. It only frightened her more. She still didn't know *who* was doing this to her. Or why.

She checked the door to make absolutely sure it was locked, turned off the TV and the lights, and went to bed, where she lay rigid and sleepless most of the night.

The night was uneventful. When Catherine awakened the next morning, it was so bright and sunny it seemed as if the terror of the previous days must have been merely a nightmare. Or just harmless pranks designed to torment Catherine about her obsession with *Lost River*.

She picked a full, flowered skirt to wear that day with a rust colored blouse. She'd bought it when Cassandra was going with Weston Fremont, who liked her to look feminine.

When she realized that she'd chosen another Cassandra-type outfit, she shoved it back into the closet.

Then she pulled it out again. She'd wear it. She'd go to school as if nothing was wrong. She couldn't start glancing behind herself every minute of the day. No. She'd act normal. Maybe her tormentor was tired of trying to scare her and had given up on it.

She was sure that's what Cassandra would do. She'd go on with her life. Her new life with Dr. Wyatt.

Catherine even tried humming a little as she combed her short hair, so like Cassandra's. She thought about Travis, Travis and her own new life.

But that made her uneasy, too, when she remembered how her mother had seemed frightened by Travis's name. Catherine had heard muffled sounds from her mother's room during the night as if she were searching for something in her closet. She probably hadn't got much sleep either.

Now was not the time to ask her about it.

After programming the VCR to tape that day's episode of *Lost River*, Catherine went to her mother's bedroom door. She listened for any noises that would indicate that she was awake, but there was only silence.

" 'Bye, Mom," Catherine whispered. Gathering up her books, she went outside, closing the outside door and checking to see that it was locked.

Liz was waiting for her in the driveway below. Catherine waved to her, but in doing so lost control of her books and dropped them on the steps.

Immediately Old Albert yelled, "Quiet!"

Catherine picked up the books, then dropped them again on purpose. Her head ached and she didn't need Old Albert on her case.

Liz giggled. "You like digging at him, don't you, Cath?"

Catherine sighed as she picked up the books again and tromped down the stairs. "No, to tell the truth I don't." She could hear the sharp edge in her voice. She didn't sound like herself. In fact she sounded like Cassandra Bly when she was upset about something.

Liz peered at her, her face bunched up with concern. "Are you okay, Cath? I thought things might be better this morning."

"I'm just tired." Catherine looked at Kade's house. His car was gone. "I guess we don't have a ride this morning."

As she spoke, she saw something lying at the end of the driveway. Right where she'd be sure to see it.

She wasn't certain at first what it was. Liz bent down to pick it up, holding it gingerly between her thumb and forefinger.

"A seat belt," she said.

Catherine felt her chest tighten. The buckle was fastened, but on one side the belt was slashed almost all the way through the cording.

"It probably fell out of Kade's car," Liz said. "You know what an advanced state of decay that wreck is in."

"Maybe." Catherine tried to believe that the severed belt had fallen out of Kade's car. But she knew it hadn't. It was cut, just like the belt the camera had focused on after Cassandra's dreadful accident.

Somebody had cut Cassandra's seat belt. Somebody who meant to harm Cassandra.

Somebody had deliberately cut this belt, too, and left it for Catherine as a reminder. Or a warning . . .

Kade could have put it there. But Catherine had a memory of him and Liz talking, making fun of the show, when that scene had played at Mr. Andersen's appliance shop. Neither he nor Liz had been looking at the screen when the camera turned toward the belt. She didn't think they even knew its significance.

"Probably fell off a trash truck," Liz said, dropping it into the gutter. "Come on, let's go to school." She started walking away.

Catherine glanced back at the house to see if Old Albert had seen them littering the street. She was sure she saw a curtain twitch.

Shivering, she followed Liz.

The day improved when they got to school. She met Travis on the stairway right after first period.

He smiled and his nice gray eyes shone with pleasure as he saw her new haircut.

"You look terrific, C.B.," he said softly.

She smiled back, unable to say anything, hating that he'd called her C.B.

Touching her arm, he turned her slightly so he could see the back of her head. "The haircut is perfect for you," he said. "You look so much like Cassandra now that you could step right into the show and take her place."

Certainly he'd meant it as a compliment, but it made Catherine shiver again. She wished she hadn't worn the Cassandra-type skirt.

"What's the matter, C.B.?" Travis asked. "Are you cold?" He moved closer as if to protect her from whatever was wrong.

Her headache was coming back. "I'm all right, Travis. But I'd rather you didn't call me C.B."

"Sorry," he said. "Does that make bad vibes?"

She tried a small laugh. "Not really. It's just that somebody calls Cassandra 'C.B.' on the show, and right now it seems as if that somebody is trying to harm her."

"I'm sorry." Travis took a step backward, looking at her. "Cathy. You look like a Cathy. Mind if I call you that?"

Nobody else called her Cathy. It would be his special name for her. "I'd like that very much," she said.

They stood there smiling at each other while kids pushed past them on their way to classes.

"I guess we should go," Catherine said.

"I'll walk you to your class." They started down the stairs. "Speaking of our soap opera, what's happening? Seemed pretty sinister the other day."

She didn't really want to talk about it, so she said, "You mean you didn't watch it yesterday?"

"I had a newspaper meeting at noon. Otherwise I would have met you at Andersen's Appliances to watch."

"I didn't go there yesterday," she said. "Kade fixed my VCR and taped the show for me. I'm taping today's episode, too."

Travis shifted his stack of books from the hip closest to her to the other hip, as if to remove an obstruction between them. "Okay if I come to your house after school and watch it?"

He was actually inviting himself over to her house. Play it cool, Catherine, she told herself. Don't melt in a little puddle right here in the hallway. All she could do was nod.

"I'll wait for you under the oak tree in front of the school," Travis said.

She didn't have a chance to say anything because Britny showed up just then.

"Travis," she said. "Where have you been? You were going to explain that trig problem to me." She eyed Catherine without greeting her. "I'll take him off your hands," she said. "I wouldn't want you to be late for cheerleading practice."

Maybe it was the fact that she knew Travis

liked her that gave Catherine the courage to defy Britny.

She linked her arm through his. "No practice today," she said. "Travis and I were discussing something important."

"Was it your soap opera?" Britny asked. "That's the only important thing in your life, isn't it, Catherine?"

"Not quite," Catherine said.

"Uh," Travis said. He sounded embarrassed. "Catherine, I did promise Britny I'd help her. We both have a study period now."

Catherine unwound her arm from his, feeling her cheeks flame.

Smiling smugly, Britny took Travis's hand and began towing him off. "I've got a key to give you," she said. "The key to the cabin."

Key to the cabin? What was going on with Travis and Britny?

Travis was looking back at Catherine. He held up the key Britny had just given him. "Our parents are good friends. We share a vacation home in the mountains. We're planning a trip up there." Pulling his other hand from Britny's, he fished a bunch of keys from his pocket and added the cabin key to the ring. Then he headed for the library study hall with Britny.

So Britny had won this round. But Travis was coming to Catherine's house after school.

Catherine told Liz all about it when they met for lunch.

"Hey," Liz said, "you invited *me* to come over and watch today's show with you. Does that mean I'm cancelled?"

Actually Catherine had invited both Liz and Kade to come and watch, in case somebody had messed with the tape again. She wanted to make sure there were witnesses this time.

"Of course you're not canceled," she said, but she could hear how halfhearted she sounded.

Liz laughed. "Wouldn't dream of intruding. Listen, I want to see today's episode. Let's go to Andersen's and watch it, then I'll head Kade off somehow so you and Travis can be alone." She winked. "Won't hurt if you've already seen it when Travis comes. Then you can watch him instead of the show."

"Liz, you're the greatest." Catherine hugged her friend briefly, then started walking. "Let's go. We've already missed the opening scene."

It didn't matter much. *Dr. Wyatt was signing Cassandra's release from the hospital. He offered to drive her home to her stepfather's mansion on the hill.*

"Fast recovery," Liz muttered.

Catherine had to admit it was, but that's the way things were in soap operas. People got over terrible injuries in days. Babies grew into school-age kids within a couple of months.

"Guess they want to get on with the romance," she said.

"Or the mystery," Liz said darkly.

Catherine felt cold again as she thought of her own personal mystery. As she remembered Dr. Wyatt's voice on her own phone.

Mr. Andersen came over to watch the show with them. "You girls got me hooked on this thing. I was telling the wife she ought to watch it, but she looks at one on another channel at noon."

Catherine wished he'd stop talking. She wanted to hear what was going on in the show.

Dr. Wyatt helped Cassandra into his little low-slung Ferrari. He fussed about, getting her settled, smoothing a blanket over her knees. Then he got in the driver's side and started the engine.

It was pleasantly dim inside the little car, and they were so close together.

"I'm afraid," Cassandra said. "My mother and James won't be home until tomorrow. I'll be alone there on the hill."

Dr. Wyatt shook his head. "I'm staying with you."

She looked at him, startled.

"You have a guest room, don't you? I'll bunk in there. You can't just be left alone."

"There are the servants," Cassandra said.

Dr. Wyatt looked at her, smiling. "Give them the night off. Tonight I'm your nurse."

"You'd better watch out for him, baby," Liz said. "You can't trust anybody right now."

Catherine was shocked. "You don't suspect Dr. Wyatt, do you? She hardly knows him."

Liz shrugged. "Maybe *she* doesn't know *him*, but it could be that *he* knows *her*. Remember, she witnessed that murder back in July, right before she had amnesia. She never did remember who the man in the dark suit was that she saw running from the scene. Maybe it was Dr. Wyatt. Maybe he's the one who took out her brakes and steering, to stop her from remembering."

"Could be," Mr. Andersen said. "It was right after she'd had amnesia that Dr. Wyatt came to Lost River General Hospital."

Liz looked up at him. "Guess you watched *Lost River* even before we got you hooked."

He looked sheepish. "Can't help but see it with all these TVs on." He went to help a customer.

"Old phony," Liz whispered. "Probably watches every soap on the channels."

"Shh," Catherine said. "Let's watch."

Cassandra and Dr. Wyatt were at the front door of the hilltop mansion now. Dr. Wyatt took Cassandra's key and opened the door, then went back to lift her from the car.

"He's going to kiss her," Liz said.

"She's not well enough," Catherine said. "Besides, you just said he might be the sicko who's been trying to kill her. He's probably going to hand her another of those bloodred roses."

The camera focused on a bunch of bloodred roses. They were in a tall white vase which stood on the console table just inside the door of the mansion.

That's where the episode ended.

Catherine stood up, chilled again. Was there going to be a rose waiting for her when she got home?

She didn't have to wait that long, because when she turned to leave the shop the first thing she saw was a whole bouquet of roses standing on a stack of boxed VCRs by the door.

A bouquet of bloodred roses.

They hadn't been there when Catherine and Liz came in.

Chapter 7

"Where did those come from?" Catherine gasped.

"Cath?" Liz took hold of her arm. "What's the matter?"

"The roses." Catherine pointed a trembling finger at the bouquet. "They weren't there before."

Liz looked at them. "You're right. They weren't. But what's the big deal? It's just a bunch of roses." She guided Catherine back to a chair. "Sit. You look as if you're going to faint. I'll find out about the roses."

Breathing raggedly, Catherine watched as Liz walked over to the cash register where Mr. Andersen was ringing up a sale. When he'd finished, both of them came back to Catherine.

"Funny thing about those roses," Mr. Andersen said. "Boy delivered them while you were watching the show. No card. Wondered who was sending me roses, but figured it was the wife. Our wedding anniversary's tomorrow. Thought it was a reminder."

Catherine felt cold. It was a reminder, all right. A reminder to *her*.

She stood up. "You can't say *those* are my imagination," she said to Liz.

Liz reached out to touch a rose as if to verify that it was real. "It's just a coincidence. Mr. Andersen, what's your wife's favorite rose?"

"Favors the Peace Rose, Vera does," Mr. Andersen said. "Likes just about any rose, though. Loves red ones."

"See?" Liz said. "They don't mean anything, Cath." She grinned at Mr. Andersen.

Catherine and Liz left the store, walking silently for half a block. Then Catherine said, "It's too much of a coincidence, Liz. A whole bouquet of *bloodred* roses?"

Liz glanced at her. "Okay, Cath. Let's say you're right. So, if things really are happening to you the way they happen to Cassandra, you've already had your surprise for the day. You don't have to worry about anything else today."

Catherine felt her breathing even out a little. Liz was right. And at least now she had a witness to something.

*   *   *

After school, Travis wasn't waiting for Catherine under the oak tree as he said he'd be. He'd probably forgotten about going to her house to watch the taped episode of *Lost River*.

Or maybe Britny had him trapped somewhere.

Dejectedly, Catherine started walking toward home. Liz had probably already headed Kade off, so there was no reason to wait for either of them.

Catherine didn't really want to be alone. She didn't want to go to her empty house. As Liz said, she'd already had her surprise for the day, but that wasn't much comfort. The person who was tormenting her didn't play by any rules.

If there *was* a person. She knew Liz still didn't believe her about the things that had happened, even after seeing — and feeling — the roses at Andersen's. She knew Liz still thought it was all her imagination, all part of her fantasy of being like Cassandra.

Maybe it was.

She was approaching Jepsen Park now. Her footsteps slowed. Would there be another tombstone there with her name on it? Uneasily her eyes scanned the expanse of green lawn and the shrubbery.

Had something moved in the bushes? Was somebody videotaping her again?

Clutching her books, she walked faster. When she suddenly heard footsteps behind her, she broke into a run.

"Cathy," someone said. "Wait."

"Travis!" Catherine whirled around, her voice breaking with relief.

"I've been trying to catch up to you," Travis said, panting a little as he reached her side. "My car won't start. I was afraid you might think I'd broken our date."

Their date. How nice that sounded. She took a moment to calm down, then said, "Sorry about your car. Want to call somebody about it?"

Travis shook his head. "I'll solve that later. I'll walk you home. The car isn't going anywhere." Fitting his stride to hers, he said, "I've been looking forward to this all day."

"Me, too," she confessed. She already knew what happened in today's episode, but she was looking forward to being with him.

It was great walking with him. He even made her laugh, talking about things at school and telling her about the accident that had laid him up the previous summer. He'd been in a Rollerblade race. His injuries weren't funny, but he made it sound as if they were.

Catherine saw Old Albert's living room curtain twitch as she and Travis walked down the driveway. She expected him to yell as they started up the stairs, and he did.

"Stop that noise," he bellowed.

"Sorry, sir," Travis called, then tiptoed elaborately up the rest of the way.

Catherine was giggling as she opened the door, which was unlocked. She'd have to remind her mother again to lock it.

It made her uneasy, and as she went inside her eyes went immediately to the small table there in the little entry hall. Cassandra had encountered more bloodred roses on the console table just inside her front door when she and Dr. Wyatt had gone into the hilltop mansion.

There was nothing on the table except a stack of advertising circulars and other mail.

"Come on in," Catherine said. "I can whip up some chocolate chip cookies, if you'd like, or we can order a pizza, or. . . ."

Her voice died away as she led him into the living room and saw the bouquet of bloodred roses in a white vase sitting on top of the TV.

She backed into Travis, almost knocking him down.

"Ooof," he grunted, grabbing her around the waist.

Any other time Catherine would have welcomed Travis's arms around her, but not at this moment. Not when she'd just spotted the roses. Not when she was alone with Travis.

Not when she clearly remembered Liz saying, "Better watch out for him, baby. You can't trust anybody right now." She'd been saying it about Dr. Wyatt on the soap opera. But Catherine couldn't trust anybody, either, could she? Had Travis been watching her from behind the bushes there in the park? Was that why she'd felt so creepy?

With these thoughts jumbling her brain, Catherine leapt away from the clutching arms, sending Travis staggering again.

"Hey, I'm sorry," he said as he regained his balance. "I didn't mean to grab you like that. I was just trying to keep from falling." He peered at her. "Hey, you're awfully pale. I really gave you a scare."

She was prepared to scream if he made any further move to touch her. But he didn't. He just stood there, meekly apologetic.

Catherine forced a laugh. "It was my fault,

Travis. I almost steamrolled you. I'm sorry."
She drew in a long, quivering breath.

"It's okay. What was it that scared you?"
He looked around, standing alert as if he were
ready to tackle whatever it was.

How much should she tell him? She didn't
want to be suspicious of him, but the strange
things hadn't started happening until the day
she met him. The day he'd said she looked
just like Cassandra.

She wished again that she could catch that
niggling little memory that had made her think
his face was familiar the first time she'd seen
him.

He stood waiting for her to tell him what
had scared her.

"It's the roses," she said, pointing at them.

Puzzled, he plucked the roses out of their
vase.

"Don't touch them!" Irrationally, Catherine
reached out to snatch them from him. She'd
forgotten about thorns. When she yanked the
roses from Travis, the thorns tore at his
fingers.

"Oh, Travis, I'm sorry," she said as several
drops of blood fell on the beige carpeting.

"Oh boy," Travis groaned. "I've stained
your carpet."

Dropping the roses, Catherine pulled a tissue from a box on the coffee table and dabbed at his wounded fingers. "My fault," she said. "I shouldn't have grabbed the roses."

Her fingers were bleeding, too, but she ignored that.

Travis looked at her, his face close to hers, as she tended his fingers. "Why did you? Grab the roses, I mean."

How much should she tell? "They reminded me of the ones on the show," she said. "You know. The red roses someone leaves for Cassandra." She avoided calling them "bloodred" roses.

"I didn't see those episodes. Are the roses something to worry about?"

"Apparently." Catherine wanted to drop the subject. She tried to remember if Travis had still been in Andersen's during the rose scene. Did that come after Britny dragged him away? Or was he lying? "Do your fingers hurt?"

"They're okay." Travis looked again at the bloodstain on the carpet. "But we'd better do something about that. Could you bring me a rag and some cold water?"

It took more than cold water to clean up the blood. Scrubbing at it made it spread out and become larger. Travis got an ice cube from the refrigerator to rub on it, but that didn't do much good, either. There was still a reddish tinge on the light-colored carpeting.

"Your mother will never let me back in your house," Travis said.

"She'll probably be too tired to notice," Catherine told him, getting to her feet and motioning for him to get up. "Look, let's forget it for now. Let's order a pizza and watch the show. Okay?"

"That *is* what I came for, isn't it?" Travis said. "I'd almost forgotten."

Catherine relaxed a little and went to the telephone to call for the pizza. While they waited, she took the bouquet of roses downstairs and deposited them in the trash.

She enjoyed watching the episode with Travis, despite her earlier fright and suspicions. She didn't tell him she'd already seen it at noon with Liz.

Travis made running comments about the show as he chewed his pizza. He recalled scenes from past shows, aired when he'd been grounded with his broken leg. He wondered aloud how other plot lines had been resolved and stopped the tape so Catherine could fill him in.

It made her feel better to talk about the improbable plot of the soap opera. It took so many twists and turns that the person who was trying to make her life follow Cassandra's would soon get discouraged and quit.

But in the back of her mind she kept seeing that bouquet of bloodred roses.

When Travis left, Catherine made sure the door was locked. She even put on the chain lock.

She forgot to undo it before her mother came home, and the chain caught, rattling the walls, when her mom tried to open the door.

"How come the big barricade?" Her mother walked wearily into the room, dropping her purse on the little table inside the door. "Is there a problem?" Easing herself onto the sofa, she kicked off her shoes.

"Sort of," Catherine said. "Travis made me promise. . . ."

"Travis!" Her mother rose slowly to her feet. "Travis was *here*?" Her tired face sagged, and her eyes searched the room, stopping at the spot on the rug. "What's that?" she asked hoarsely.

"Mom, it's just a little blood. You see, Travis. . . ."

Her mother put her hands up on either side of her face. "Oh, no," she whispered. "Oh, no, no, no. It's starting all over again."

Chapter 8

Catherine rushed forward to grab her mother's arm. "Mom," she said, "what's the matter?"

Her mother swayed a little. She stared at the blotchy red spot on the carpet.

"Mom, sit down." Catherine had never seen her like this. She didn't know what to do. Should she call somebody? Who? Kade? Old Albert? 911?

Her mother sat. She turned her eyes to Catherine. "You're absolutely sure it was *Travis*?" she said in a hoarse whisper.

"Yes, Mom, I'm sure. Travis Cavanaugh. You know, the new guy I was telling you about?" She sat beside her mother, rubbing one of her arms. She couldn't think what else to do.

Her mother dropped her hands from her face. "Oh. Travis *Cavanaugh!*" She exhaled, as if she'd been holding her breath for a long time. "Cavanaugh. Yes. I remember your telling me about him." Turning to look at Catherine she said, "What was he doing here?"

"He walked me home, Mom. We're friends. He watched *Lost River* last year when he had to lie around a lot with a broken leg. He came here to watch today's episode with me."

"Oh." Her mom managed a shaky smile. "That's nice, honey. I'm glad you've got a new friend." She seemed more like herself now. "What about Kade? Isn't he a little bent out of shape about having some other guy hanging around?"

"Kade doesn't own me, Mom. We're just friends."

"He likes you a lot. Be sure you don't hurt him." Her mother reached out now and smoothed back Catherine's hair.

Catherine thought about how she'd already hurt Kade, but she didn't say anything about that. "We're just *friends*, Kade and I. He's like a brother."

Her mother got to her feet and walked over to peer down at the pinkish spot where Travis had dripped blood. "Be nice to Kade, Catherine." She paused, staring at the spot, then walked back to the sofa. "Tell me how the blood got there."

She looked so tired that Catherine didn't

want to burden her with the whole story of the strange things that had been going on. She tried on a grin that almost worked. "Travis got too close to some thorns, Mom. That's all."

Her mother gave her a soft smile. "So he's already bringing you roses."

Catherine let that go. "I'll fix you something to eat, Mom. Travis and I had pizza. There's some left."

"Thanks anyway, but I ate at the cafeteria again." She stood up. "Think I'll go relax in a hot bath. Anything good on TV tonight?"

"I'll check." Catherine picked up the program listing.

"Maybe I should watch the tape of *Lost River*," her mother said. "What am I missing?"

"Not a whole lot," Catherine said quickly. She didn't want to watch the show again. She didn't want to see Cassandra's face as she saw the bloodred roses waiting for her. She knew exactly how Cassandra had felt — the anxiety, the fear, the sheer terror of knowing someone was trying to frighten her, maybe do more harm to her. "Let's watch something else."

"All right. You get it set up." Her mother started again toward her bedroom.

"Mom." There were some more questions that hadn't been answered yet. "Mom, what was it that upset you so much about the bloodstain on the carpet?"

Her mother gave a little laugh. "Oh, that. It's just that I don't know how we'll explain it to Old Albert."

"But what did you mean when you said 'It's starting all over again?'"

Her mother shrugged. "Like I said, we'll have to start explaining things all over again to Old Albert. Don't you remember how he got upset about every little spot when we first moved in?" She yawned. "On second thought, I think I'll go right to bed after my bath. See you in the morning, honey."

"Mom, one more thing."

Her mother turned slightly, but not all the way.

"Mom, why did the name Travis spook you so much?"

Her mother took a while to answer, as if she were considering what to say. She didn't look at Catherine. "I already told you. I used to know a young man by the name of Travis. That's all."

She went on into her room and closed the door.

Catherine knew it was useless to try to get her to say more. But there was something she wasn't telling. Did it have anything to do with the way she'd been thumping around in her closet last night? What was she looking for?

Or had she been trying to *hide* something?

The next day, Catherine was surprised when Britny came up to her after English class and beckoned her to a spot under the stairwell where they wouldn't be trampled by other kids.

"Catherine," she said, "I just want you to know that I don't mind if Travis takes you home now and then. He's felt kind of out of things, being new here and all. I'm happy that he's making some new friends."

Who did she think she was, the queen of England, granting Catherine a royal favor? "He doesn't seem so out of things," Catherine said stiffly. "He's already on the newspaper. He has a lot of friends."

Britny nodded. "Yes. But when they get to know him, they might . . ." She looked around as if checking to see if anyone was listening. "You know. His *problem*. I feel kind of responsible for him. I've known him since we were kids."

"His *problem*?" Catherine stared at Britny. "What are you talking about?"

Britny raised her eyebrows. "You mean he hasn't told you yet?

"The only problem I know about is that he broke his leg and was laid up for a while a year ago. Is that it?" The way Britny kept looking furtively around disturbed Catherine.

Britny put her hand on Catherine's arm. "It wasn't his broken leg that kept him home watching soap operas for so long, dear." She turned suddenly, smiling brightly at one of her friends who was coming toward them. Leaning close to Catherine, she whispered, "Don't tell him I told you. It makes him . . . you know." Turning back to her friend, she said, "Well hi, Marty. I was waiting for you."

Catherine grabbed her arm. "Britny, stay here a minute," she hissed. "Tell me about this 'problem.'"

Britny raised her eyebrows. "Ask Travis," she whispered. "He really shouldn't keep something like that from you."

Pulling her arm away from Catherine, she walked off with Marty.

Catherine watched her go. Was Britny trying to scare her away from Travis? Or had she honestly thought she should warn her about something? It seemed unlikely that she'd care what happened to Catherine. Britny had never done a nice thing for her since they were in the fourth grade and had started competing for the same things.

Catherine knew Britny was not above lying.

On the other hand, Britny had known Travis for a long time. Their families were friends. She was probably genuinely interested in his welfare.

Perplexed, Catherine went on to her next class.

At noon she was waiting for Liz when Travis came charging through the crowds in the hallway as if he was looking for her. "Hi," he said with a smile that almost destroyed her. "How about we run uptown to Andersen's and watch today's episode of *Lost River*. You've got me hooked on it again."

"It *is* kind of exciting right now." She stalled, thinking about his "problem." If it was as serious as Britny seemed to indicate, was she safe going anywhere with him? She remembered her suspicions of the previous day.

"Well?" Travis cocked his head to one side, waiting.

What could happen on a trip uptown?

"Sure," she said, just as Liz came pushing through the crowds. "Want to go with us to Andersen's to watch *Lost River*?" she asked.

Liz looked from Catherine to Travis and back to Catherine. "I'll pass. I want to grab a bite, then hit the library. Got a mega-report coming up." Winking at Catherine, she started walking off down the hall. "See you after school."

"Not today," Catherine called. "I'm supposed to meet with Suzanne and Erin in the auditorium to plan a little cheerleading routine we're doing for the next assembly."

"Okay," Liz said cheerfully. "Call you later." She joined the tide of students flowing toward the lunchroom.

Catherine turned back to Travis, feeling a little flustered. His brown eyes were clear as he looked down at her. He certainly didn't seem like a guy with a "problem." Britny was the one with a problem.

"We'd better hurry," Travis said. "Wouldn't want to miss anything."

They met Kade just outside the big front doors. "Off to watch the soap?" he asked.

"Yeah," Travis said. "Want to join us?"

Kade shook his head. "Don't think so. Not today." He looked at Catherine. "Let me know if there are any more bloodred roses," he said as he left.

"Let's go," Catherine said to Travis. Forget Kade.

The episode that day was scary.

Dr. Wyatt settled Cassandra in her big, beau-

tiful bedroom. Pulling the heavy drapes closed, he said, "I want you to sleep for a while. I'll go get you some hot milk to help you relax."

Cassandra leaned back against the pile of pillows behind her. "Thank you, Carlton." There was a contented purr in her voice. "I really am tired."

It always amazed Catherine that people in soap operas slept half sitting, propped up with three or four pillows. Maybe that was to keep their faces from sagging if they lay flat. They had to look good for the camera.

"How's she going to sleep with all those pillows?" Travis said.

Catherine laughed. It soothed her, to have Travis thinking the same silly thoughts as she was. Whatever his "problem" was, it didn't affect his sense of humor.

Dr. Wyatt left the room. Cassandra reclined there in the big bed, smiling in the soft lamplight.

Catherine leaned back in the chair Mr. Andersen had brought for her. She felt herself slipping into the show, becoming Cassandra. She smiled, waiting, knowing Dr. Wyatt — Carlton — would be back again in a few minutes.

Then, without warning, Cassandra's lamp

went out. Her bedroom was plunged into darkness.

Catherine gasped at the same time Cassandra did. Out of the corner of her eye she saw Travis glance at her.

"Carlton?" *Cassandra called out into the darkness.* "Carlton?"

There was no sound.

In a voice-over, Cassandra said, "The light-bulb probably blew. Or maybe Carlton plugged in the toaster or something and it blew a fuse."

"Carlton?" *she called again.* "Carlton?"

No answer.

A deodorant commercial came on.

Travis groaned. "That's what I like about the soaps. Just when things are most suspenseful, we take a look at people's armpits."

Catherine nodded. She hoped Travis hadn't thought she was crazy, gasping the way she'd done when the lights went out. But it had been frightening. She'd felt as if she was there, inside of Cassandra.

Keeping her voice calm, she said, "Want to bet that when we get back to the show, they'll go off on some other story line, leaving us hanging?"

She was right. After the commercial the

show went to a totally different story line. But just at the end, it came back to Cassandra.

She was in total blackness. It had been a long time since Dr. Wyatt left. She was still calling for him.

In the darkness, a door creaked open.

"Funny," Travis said. "That door didn't creak when they came in."

Catherine was definitely feeling uneasy. Were the lights at her apartment going to go out that night? Was a door going to creak open as she stared blindly into the darkness?

No. How could anyone shut off the apartment lights? The fuse boxes were in Old Albert's basement. He kept the place locked up like a fortress.

No. This was one episode that wouldn't be repeated.

Not unless it was Old Albert who was trying to scare her.

Yeah, right.

Well, she told herself, if the lights did go out, at least she'd know who was doing it.

Cassandra said, "Who's there? Tell me! Is that you, Carlton?"

No answer.

Then Cassandra said, "Roses. I smell roses."

And a whispery, soft voice said, "Of course you do, C.B. Roses. For your funeral."

That's where the episode ended.

"A real cliffhanger," Mr. Andersen said.

Catherine hadn't even been aware that he'd been watching the program with her and Travis. But there he was, in back of them, leaning against a pile of boxes containing VCRs.

With a smile, Mr. Andersen said, "I knew from the start that the roses were bad news."

"A nice touch today," Travis said. "An odor can be as scary as something seen or heard."

Catherine thought of the dim, empty apartment she'd be going home to. "Want to check my place for more roses after school?" she asked Travis, trying to keep her voice light as if she meant it as a joke.

"Love to," he said. "It's been a while since I've been asked to slay dragons." He spoke as if he'd been out of action for a long time. Catherine wondered if this was the time to ask him about his problem. No, she'd ask him when they were at her house. That way he'd have time to explain it.

"Meet me at my apartment after I take care of the cheerleader business," she told him.

"No, I'll give you a ride home. The car's fixed." Travis said. "I'll wait in the library. I need to study anyway."

"Okay," Catherine said, standing up and folding her chair. "That would be nice."

On her way to the auditorium after her last class, Catherine met Kade.

"Want a ride home?" he asked.

"Thanks," she said. "But I have a cheer-leading practice."

He shrugged. "So I'll wait. I don't mind."

"No." Catherine wondered how she should say this. "Kade, I appreciate the offer, but really, I don't want you to wait."

His eyes narrowed. "Got a ride already?"

She nodded.

"Okay," he said. "Okay." He looked at her for a moment. "How well do you know Travis?"

"How do you know that's who I have a ride with?"

He shifted from one foot to the other. "Cath," he said.

She waited.

"Forget it," he said. "Look, I'll call you tonight."

He loped off down the hall.

Kids were streaming from the school as Catherine headed for the auditorium. She didn't see Suzanne and Erin. But the door was unlocked, so she went inside.

The huge room was cavernous and vacant. In the dim light, she walked down an aisle and climbed the stairs to the stage. It was empty except for a couple of chairs, a pile of coiled electrical cords, and a low bench that must have been part of a stage set at one time.

She looked around. Maybe they needed more than three cheerleaders to perform on that big stage. Maybe they should use the whole squad. They wouldn't want their little act to look puny.

She was standing in the middle of the big stage, looking out toward the rows of empty seats, when the dim light went out.

She was in total darkness.

Terror engulfed her. "Hey," she yelled. "Turn on the lights."

Maybe it was just somebody shutting down everything at the end of the day.

Taking a couple of deep breaths to put down her fright, Catherine called, "Hello? We need the lights for a while. Is anybody there?"

Silence.

A scene replayed in Catherine's mind. She saw Cassandra sitting against her pillows, her eyes straining into the darkness.

"Oh, no," Catherine whispered.

It was at that moment that she smelled the sweet odor of roses.

Chapter 9

Catherine screamed.

She couldn't help it. The terror squeezed it out of her lungs, pumping air up through her throat past her vocal cords and spilling screams from her lips. Again and again she screamed.

Over the sound of her own screams she heard someone whispering. At first the words were meaningless. She heard only the hoarse sibilance of the whispering voice in the darkness. Only the hiss of air as if someone's mouth was too close to a microphone. The whisper filled the cavernous auditorium, echoing back from the far corners, teasing Catherine's eardrums with feathers of sound.

Her screams faded into a whimper, and she ran forward. She had to find her way out of this place, away from the suffocating stink of roses, away from the bodyless whispering.

Then there were words.

"C.B.," the whispering voice said. "C.B. Don't run. The rim of the world is out there in the darkness."

Catherine stopped, trying to organize her spinning senses. The warning was real. The edge of the stage must be somewhere there in front of her. She didn't know how far. One more step and she might plunge into dark nothingness.

"Who are you?" she gasped into the blackness. "Why are you doing this to me?"

"Don't you know?" the Whisperer asked.

"No." Catherine turned slowly, trying to locate the direction of the whispering. But it was everywhere. It must be coming over the sound system.

"No," she repeated, her voice trembling. "I don't know."

The Whisperer gave a deep-throated laugh. The small explosions of sound over the microphone were more terrifying than the words.

"Please," Catherine whimpered. "Please." That was the only word she could find. The scent of the roses was making her sick. In another minute or two her knees were going to buckle.

She was going to fall.

"Do you like the roses, C.B.?" the Whisperer asked. "The bloodred roses?"

Catherine swayed. Which way was the edge of the stage now? She'd lost track of it when she'd turned.

If she toppled forward, would she go over the edge? Over the rim of the world? Would that be the end?

"Please."

There was a moment of silence, then a loud, intense whisper. "Catherine! Watch out!"

She jumped to one side, sobbing with terror.

There was a sharp pain in one shin, and then she was falling, falling, falling into darkness.

She screamed.

Then it was over, and she realized she hadn't fallen off the stage. Merely to the floor, which was bad enough because she felt blood where her shin had struck something.

She put out a hand and felt the low bench she'd seen before the lights went out. She'd tripped over it.

"Please," she whispered hopelessly.

She was answered by silence.

Then a door opened, and pale light from the corridor seeped into the auditorium. It wasn't much, but enough for Catherine to see that she lay right on the lip of the stage. Another step and she would have gone over.

That's what the Whisperer had intended for her to do when he told her to watch out. She was sure of it.

Someone said, "Hey, how come it's dark in here? Wasn't this where we were supposed to meet?"

It was Erin's voice. Erin. One of the other cheerleaders who'd been assigned to work up the routine.

Then Suzanne spoke. "Maybe Cath cancelled out entirely. What did her note say?"

Before Erin could answer, Catherine gasped out, "Erin? Suzanne? Help me."

"Where are you?" In the dim light from the corridor Catherine could see Erin put her hand above her eyes and peer around the big room.

Catherine tried to say something but choked on the words.

"How come you're in the dark?" Suzanne began groping her way along the back wall toward the switch for the utility light. "You got somebody up there with you?"

Erin laughed and made kissy noises.

As soon as the utility light came on, Catherine scrambled to her feet and ran down the steps at the far side of the stage. Her muscles were stiff and rigid, and she still felt as if she might fall again.

Erin and Suzanne were coming down the aisle.

"Phew," Erin said. "Who sprayed rose air freshener in here? It's really strong."

"Hey, stay there," Suzanne called to Catherine. "Aren't we going to work on our routine on the stage?"

Catherine hurtled down the aisle to meet them. Now that she was safe, her whole body trembled. "Not now," she managed to say. She took hold of Suzanne's hand, needing to touch warm human flesh. "Look, I'm a little shook up. Somebody turned out the lights. I almost fell off the stage."

Suzanne looked up toward the sound room. "They probably didn't know you were here. Why didn't you call out?"

"I did." Catherine stopped. Would they believe her if she told them about the Whisperer? Didn't everybody in the school know by now that she was having hallucinations because of the soap opera she watched? "Let's get out of here," she said.

"What about our rehearsal?" Erin asked.

"Some other time." Catherine let go of Suzanne's hand and hurried from the auditorium, not caring if the other girls came with her or not. She heard them whispering to each other as they followed her.

Out in the well-lighted corridor Catherine leaned against the wall to stop her trembling.

"Hey," Suzanne said, "your leg is bleeding."

"I tripped." Catherine didn't feel like explaining. "Look, I heard you mention a note from me. Who gave it to you?"

"Nobody," Erin said. "It was taped to my locker."

"What did it say?"

Erin looked puzzled. "You losing it, old girl? Can't remember what your own note said?"

Catherine sucked in a deep breath of air. It seemed as if she'd never get the stench of roses out of her lungs. "I didn't write any note," she said.

Erin's eyes grew large. "What do you mean?"

Catherine shook her head. "Nothing. It's okay. I'm all right now. Did you recognize the handwriting on the note?"

"It was typed." Erin riffled through the pages of one of the books she carried and pulled out a sheet of typing paper. "Here it is." She looked curiously at Catherine.

The note said, *Erin and Suzanne: Something came up. Go have a Pepsi and meet me at 3:30 instead of 3:00. Catherine.*

It was badly typed. The words ran all the

way to the right margin, and there were four strikeovers. Whoever had done it probably had never taken a typing class.

Or maybe someone just wanted it to appear that way.

It probably wasn't a useful clue.

"May I keep this?" Catherine asked, holding up the sheet of paper.

"It's yours," Erin said. "Cath, are you sure you're okay? You look kind of washed out. And you'd better do something about your leg. It's bleeding all over." She pulled a tissue from her purse and handed it to Catherine.

Dabbing at the blood on her leg Catherine said, "Thanks. I'll be okay." She pushed herself away from the wall and started walking unsteadily down the corridor. "But if you don't mind, I'd rather rehearse that routine tomorrow."

She heard Suzanne and Erin whispering again as she left. She couldn't do anything about that. She had to get home and lie down. She could have been badly hurt if she'd fallen off the stage.

It wasn't until she was climbing the stairs to her apartment that she remembered Travis was going to wait for her in the school library. She should have gone there and found him.

He would have driven her home and he'd be here with her now.

She opened the screen door. The apartment door was locked. Good. Her mother had remembered to do it.

She got out her key and opened it, remembering the day before when Travis had been there with her.

An unbidden thought came into her mind. Travis had been at school while her terrifying experience in the auditorium was going on.

Could he have been the Whisperer?

Who else knew she'd be in the auditorium right after school?

Well, Kade knew. Liz. Britny. Suzanne and Erin. There was also a sign-up sheet somewhere that showed who would be using what facilities at what times. Anybody could have known.

Probably the only person who *didn't* know that she'd be in the auditorium at 3:00 P.M. was Old Albert.

The phone rang, shattering Catherine's nerves, making her drop her books as she stood there just inside the apartment door.

Old Albert thumped on the ceiling below.

The phone rang four times before Catherine could slow down her breathing enough to answer it. What if it was Dr. Carlton Wyatt's voice again?

The caller was Travis.

"Cathy." He sounded worried. "Are you okay?"

She drew in a deep breath. "Yes."

"I met Erin and Suzanne when I went looking for you," Travis said. "They told me you were upset about something."

"Yes." That was all Catherine could manage.

"Did it have something to do with what happened on *Lost River* today?"

"Yes."

"Cathy." His voice held authority now. "Lock your door. Stay right there in your apartment. I'll be right over."

"Okay, Travis." Catherine felt weak. She had no will to resist whatever he said. She was like Cassandra, giving in to what Dr. Carlton Wyatt told her to do.

"Don't open your door to *anybody* until I get there." Travis hung up.

Maybe she shouldn't open the door to him, either.

From where she stood Catherine could see Kade's car turning into his driveway.

So he hadn't gone directly home from

school, either. *He* could have been the Whisperer in the auditorium. He helped a lot with the sound and projection equipment.

She turned away from the window. Was Kade looking up there at her?

Frightened, she hurried to the doorway of her mother's bedroom, with some idea of hiding in mind.

The room was always orderly, unlike Catherine's. The bed was smoothly made, the jars and bottles on her dresser nicely arranged, the books on her bedside table stacked neatly.

Catherine walked into the room, needing to smell her mother's scent, needing the closeness of her things. She sat down on the bed, noting the title of the top book on the little table. It was a mystery novel entitled *A Slight Case of Murder*.

Then she saw something else. There was a coverless box pushed partially under the bed. Curious, she leaned over to look inside. On top were tattered copies of the first books that Catherine remembered: *Little Red Riding Hood,* and *The Three Little Pigs.* Her mother used to read them to her. In her memory, she could still hear her mother saying in a deep wolf-voice, "Little pig, little pig, let me come in." She remembered how scared she used to be, how she shivered when her mother read those words because she knew the wolf wanted to eat the pigs.

Underneath the books was an album. It had a deep maroon cover with gold lettering that said simply PHOTOGRAPHS.

Catherine picked it up. There was something familiar about it. She'd seen it before, but not for a long, long time. That was odd because her mother loved to flip through the other photo albums filled with pictures of the two of them with Catherine's father, when he was alive. She'd talk about the good times they'd had, the places they'd gone, the things they'd done. The photos were all neatly labeled, with names and dates.

Catherine ran her fingers over the smooth maroon cover. She tried to recall the last time she'd held the album. She'd been sitting on the floor in this very room. There'd been boxes all around. It must have been when she and her mother had moved in, after the death of her father.

She squeezed her eyes shut, trying to force the memory. She'd found the album in a box, had lifted it out, had sat down to turn its pages.

She felt uncomfortable, remembering. Something had happened. She'd been turning the pages, just as she was now, peering at the pictures of her mother as a young girl.

Now she turned the pages again, one after another. She remembered seeing some of the pictures of her mother with her girlfriends. *Lucy and I at the lake* it said under one of the pictures. *Lucy and I dressed for the prom*, it said under another.

Catherine turned another page, and looked straight down into Travis's face. A full page photograph of Travis.

The suddenness of seeing him made her gasp. He grinned at her from the page, his face turned a little sideways, his eyes gazing into hers.

Catherine felt sick. She remembered something. She'd been looking at this picture that other time when her mother had come into the room and snatched the book away from her. Mom had slammed it shut and put it back in the box, saying that this was not something Catherine wanted to look at. She'd got a chair and put the box on the top shelf of her closet.

This must have been what she was looking for the night Catherine had heard her thumping around in the closet, the night she'd first mentioned Travis.

Catherine swallowed the fear that choked her and lowered her eyes to the neatly printed label below the picture. *Travis*, it said.

But that was impossible. Travis wasn't even born when her mother was a young girl.

Quickly Catherine turned another page. The next one was filled with small snapshots of her mother and Travis. The two of them standing on top of a mountain with other mountains falling away behind them. The two of them walking home from school, carrying their books on their hips, like Travis had done the other day.

But what was he doing with her mother? Was she in some kind of time warp or something?

Catherine was turning the next page when there was a soft knock at the outside door.

Her heart rattling, she shrank back against the headboard of the bed.

The next knock was louder.

"Catherine," Travis called. "Catherine, let me come in."

Catherine felt paralyzed, remembering again her mother's voice, lowered to imitate the wolf calling to the three little pigs. "Little pig, little pig, let me come in."

She cowered on the bed, covering her ears with her hands.

Even so, she could still hear Travis. "Catherine," he called, his voice becoming urgent. "Catherine. Let me come in."

"Not by the hair on my chinny-chin-chin," she whispered.

Chapter 10

Catherine wasn't sure how long she lay that way, ears covered, eyes squeezed shut, breath coming in jerky sobs. What did Travis want? Why was his picture in her mother's album?

Travis continued to pound on the door and yell her name. "Catherine! Catherine!"

If he'd just stop saying it that way, she might open the door. If she didn't, would he huff and puff and blow her house in?

She had no proof that he was the Whisperer.

But she also had no proof that he wasn't.

She wouldn't let him come in.

Suddenly Old Albert joined in. "Stop that noise!" he bellowed.

There was silence for a moment, then Catherine heard Travis's feet running down the stairs. He was leaving.

"Thank you, Old Albert," she whispered aloud. "Thank you."

Old Albert would send him away and then probably come up and pound on her door to screech at her not ever to let that happen again. And she'd grab him around the neck and kiss his leathery old cheek in sheer gratitude. He'd faint from surprise.

Stiffly, Catherine got up from the bed and stood in the middle of the floor. Her breath still came in jerks, but her heart was slowing down a little now. Maybe she should call her mother and ask her to come home early. She didn't want to be there alone.

The album was still on the floor at her feet where she'd dropped it. It had fallen open to the picture of Travis. Not wanting to touch it, Catherine reached out with her toe to flip the book shut.

But before she could get it closed, she heard footsteps again. Two sets of footsteps.

Who was coming?

There was a low rumble of voices, one anxious and urgent, the other grumbling and annoyed.

Travis and Old Albert. Travis was coming back up the stairs, bringing Old Albert with him.

Catherine heard the jangle of keys and knew what was happening. Travis had convinced Old Albert that something was wrong in the apartment because Catherine didn't answer. Old Albert had got his master key and was going to let Travis in.

Why hadn't she used the time to barricade the door? Maybe she could still get the chain attached.

She ran into the living room, but it was too late. The door was already opening.

"Catherine!" Travis exclaimed when he saw her. "Why didn't you open up?"

She must have looked poised for flight because he rushed over and grabbed her arm.

"Are you okay?" His voice sounded hoarse with concern. "I thought something had happened to you."

Old Albert stood there glaring at her. "Better be a good explanation for this," he growled. "Young feller near battered the door down." He went over to inspect for damage. "I don't want any more of this. First the railing and now the door."

"I . . . I . . . I," Catherine stammered. What could she say?

Travis stared at her. "Cathy, has something happened? Is somebody here?"

Letting go of her arm, he dashed around the

122

apartment, looking in Catherine's room, in the small kitchen, in her mother's room.

He came back carrying the album, open at the page with his picture. His face showed total bewilderment.

"What's this?" he asked softly.

Old Albert craned his neck to see. "Any dunce can see what it is," he said. "It's you."

"This is *not* me," Travis said.

"But it says right there that it's you." Reaching out a trembling hand, Catherine pointed at where her mother had neatly printed *Travis* at the bottom of the photo.

Travis shook his head. "It's *not* me." Bringing the album closer to his face he studied the picture. "For one thing, look at the hair. I'd never wear a cut like that. Looks like the sixties. And those moles. Look." He pointed at a cheek mole, then at one near the right eyebrow of the photographed face. "Do you see anything like that on me?"

Catherine looked at the picture. She looked at Travis. "No," she said. But those things could be removed, couldn't they?

Old Albert peered from one face to the other. Finally he shrugged. "I don't know what's going on. Just don't make any more noise. And don't wreck any more of my possessions or you'll pay for them."

With a disgusted look at both Catherine and Travis, he turned and stumped back down the stairs.

Catherine wanted to ask him to stay. But what could she say? He'd probably think whatever she said was nonsense.

She was left alone with Travis.

Her heart rattling, Catherine looked at him. His face was bunched into a troubled frown as he looked at the photograph.

"This has to be my uncle," he said. "Mom always said I looked just like him."

He seemed genuinely troubled.

Catherine kept her distance, staying between Travis and the door, which seemed miles away. "Your uncle," she said. "Don't you know for sure?"

Travis shook his head. "He died when he wasn't much older than I am now." Closing the album, he looked at the front cover. "Whose album is this, anyway?"

"My mother's," Catherine said.

"Hasn't she ever told you anything about this picture?"

"No. I've never seen it before." The old memory jiggled in her brain. "Well, I saw it once. When we moved in here. I saw that picture and asked who it was. Mom grabbed the album away from me and put it in a box on the top shelf of her closet."

That was why Travis had seemed vaguely familiar to her when she'd first seen him. She'd wondered all those years ago why her mother didn't want her looking at that picture, and the memory of it had stayed in her mind. It had tried to surface the day she'd met Travis.

Travis still studied the photo. "Didn't she ever tell you what happened to him?"

"No." Catherine wasn't sure she wanted to hear.

"He was murdered," Travis said.

Catherine's knees buckled and she staggered the few steps to the sofa. "Murdered," she whispered.

Murder happened only to people in movies. Or in soap operas.

But it had happened to this other Travis, this Travis that her mother had known.

It could happen to Catherine.

Her mind darted down avenues she didn't care to explore. What had this other Travis been to her mother?

Without ever meaning to, without even realizing she was going to, Catherine began to sob. Travis was instantly beside her on the sofa.

"Oh, Cathy." His face drooped with remorse. "I didn't mean to upset you. I shouldn't have told you about my uncle."

She tried to control her voice. "It's okay. My mother probably would have told me about it if I'd asked."

She dug into a pocket of her jeans, fished out a tattered tissue and scrubbed her nose. "It's just that I don't know what's going on." She sniffed a couple of times, then said, "Travis, something weird happened today."

She watched his face closely as she told him what had happened in the auditorium. She got no clues from it.

"The whisper in the darkness, just like what happened to Cassandra on today's *Lost River* episode," he said.

She nodded. "And the smell of roses."

"It couldn't have been planned ahead of time," he said. "The person had to have watched today's episode. Then he saw an opportunity when you went to the auditorium. Do you know who was still around after school?"

She shook her head mournfully. "No, except for you. I thought it might have been you. That's why I didn't want to open the door."

Travis reached for her, tucking her head down onto his shoulder and letting her cry until her sobs turned into soft hiccups, like a dumb little kid.

Then he held her out so he could look into her eyes.

"Cathy," he said. "It wasn't me. Believe me. But we'll figure out who's doing this to you."

Relief that somebody finally believed what she said warmed Catherine. She felt her doubts about Travis begin to fade. "I feel as if I'm *living* in a soap opera. It's scary."

"Poor Cathy," he said.

He reached out a hand to smooth back a lock of her hair. "Look, let's go out and get something to eat. Then we'll come back here and I'll stay with you until your mother gets home."

"Okay." Maybe it was the way he called her Cathy that made her trust him again. Her dad had called her that when she was little. Before he died.

Travis stood up, pulling her up with him. "I know a place called the Mazatlan that serves the best burritos in the world."

He took her to a small restaurant with such a nice feel to it that she began to relax. The brightly painted chairs and the fireplace in one corner made it seem friendly and safe.

While they ate the humongous burritos,

they went over the details of that day's *Lost River* episode, then what had happened in the auditorium. It was all beginning to sound unreal, even to Catherine.

Travis watched her thoughtfully. She wasn't sure if he believed all of it.

Before he could say anything, Kade and Liz walked into the small restaurant.

That was odd. Kade was a McDonald's person who could live on burgers and fries forever. Catherine had never known him to eat Mexican food. And Liz. She didn't like anything spicy.

But Catherine didn't follow them every moment of the day. They could both be tortilla freaks for all she knew.

Liz's eyes swept the room as if she were looking for someone. When she saw Catherine and Travis, she came right to their table, with Kade following behind.

"Well, look who's here," Liz said in a fake cheery voice.

Kade didn't say anything. He nodded at Catherine, glanced at Travis, then looked at the enormous sombrero that decorated the wall behind them. Obviously it didn't make him happy to see the two of them together.

"Kade and I are studying for a psych exam,"

Liz went on. "Thought we needed a bite or two to work up a little energy."

She kept looking Catherine in the eye as if she wanted to convey some message. But Catherine wasn't getting it. What was she trying to say?

"Want to join us?" Travis asked politely.

Liz shook her head. "Thanks, but we wouldn't be good company, what with neuroses and psychoses on our minds." She looked at Catherine as if that should mean something.

Catherine frowned slightly, trying to tell Liz her message wasn't getting through.

Liz gave up. "Enjoy your burritos," she said. "See you later." She turned toward Kade, then turned back again. "Hey, did you see your soap today? It sure looks like curtains for Cassandra." She giggled nervously. "Sounds like the title of a murder mystery, doesn't it? *Curtains for C.B.*"

Once again she looked into Catherine's eyes, glanced at Travis, then back to Catherine. Was she sending a warning? About Travis? Did Liz know something that Catherine didn't?

Kade put a hand on Liz's arm. "They've found us a table."

"We'll be seeing you," Liz said as they left.

Travis twitched his head in their direction. "They an item?"

"No," Catherine said. She was still wondering what Liz had been trying to tell her.

But Travis's gray eyes were clear as he gazed at her.

She smiled at him. "Well, maybe they *are* an item. Who knows?"

It had surprised her to see Liz and Kade together. As far as she knew, they'd never been together before without her.

It bothered her. Not so much that they were together, but that if Liz had come to give her a message, how had she known where to come?

Could her apartment be bugged? Could Kade or Liz or both of them have been listening in and heard Travis mention where they were going?

She and Travis finished their burritos and headed back to Catherine's apartment. She was still a little nervous about being alone in his car with him, but she tried to overcome that by looking at the personal touches he'd added to it. He'd replaced the standard steering wheel with a polished wooden one, and the top of the console gearshift had a hand-carved wooden head of a dog. The gas pedal was like a large foot, with toes.

"Pretty," she said, touching the top of the gearshift.

"I made that while I — " He hesitated. "While my busted leg healed," he finished.

What had he been going to say?

Catherine took a deep breath. "How long did it take your leg to heal?"

"A long time," he said, keeping his eyes straight ahead. "A long time."

She knew he wasn't going to tell her about his "problem," at least not that night.

Catherine's mother was home when they got there. She was standing in the middle of the living room, holding the album they'd left on the sofa.

"How did this get out here in the living room?" she asked without greeting them.

"Mom," Catherine said, "I wasn't snooping. I'll tell you about that later. But both Travis and I are wondering about a picture in it. The one that looks like Travis."

Her mother gazed at the two of them for what seemed like a long time before she said, "His name was Travis, too. Travis Jalinsky. Everybody called him T.J."

"Jalinsky was my mother's maiden name," Travis said.

"Yes. Your mother was Travis's sister." Catherine's mom looked down at the photograph. "I guess you had to find out someday." She opened the album to the picture labeled Travis. Her face was sad as she looked at it. "We were planning to be married, T.J. and I."

"Mom," Catherine said, "Travis told me that his Uncle Travis was murdered."

Her mother raised her eyes and looked straight at Catherine. "Yes. I was the one who killed him."

Chapter 11

Catherine stared at her mother in disbelief.

She had to be kidding.

But who would kid about something that hideous?

"Mom," Catherine said, her voice sounding hoarse and unfamiliar to her own ears.

Her mother turned away as if she couldn't bear to have Catherine look at her.

"Mrs. Belmont. . . ." Travis began.

Catherine's mother took a deep breath and turned back to face them. "Oh, I didn't pull the trigger. That was somebody else. But it was my fault. It was *because* of me that T.J. was murdered."

She swayed a little, and Catherine rushed to her side. She took the album from her and eased her down onto the sofa. She sat beside her. "Tell us what happened, Mom."

Travis pulled up a chair so that he sat close enough to touch Catherine's mother. But he didn't reach out.

She looked at him. "Your mother never told you about me." It was a statement rather than a question.

"No," he said. "Not about you. All I've ever known is that my uncle was murdered by someone named Joe Sims."

Catherine's mother drew in a deep breath. "Does your mother know I live here in this town?"

Travis shook his head. "I don't know, Mrs. Belmont. She's never mentioned you."

Catherine's mother looked at him silently for a moment, then said, "Then you didn't go out of your way to get acquainted with my daughter just because you knew she was connected to me."

For a moment Travis looked as if he didn't understand. Then his eyes widened. "Mrs. Belmont, I swear to you that the only reason I wanted to get to know Cathy is that I think she's a terrific girl. We met at Andersen's while she and her friends were watching *Lost River* on TV."

Again Catherine's mother looked at him silently. Then she asked, "What were you doing in the appliance shop at noon on a school day?"

"Britny dragged me there," Travis said. "Our families are old friends, and we've known each other for a long time. I was helping her pick out some CD equipment."

Catherine's mother's face softened. "I'm sorry, Travis. I didn't mean to put you on trial."

"That's okay," Travis said politely.

"One more question?" Catherine's mother said.

"Sure."

"This Britny. Is her mother's name Tessa?" She fidgeted nervously with an earring while she waited for him to answer.

Travis looked puzzled. "Her name's Louise."

Catherine's mother seemed relieved.

"Who's Tessa, Mom?" Catherine asked.

Her mother shrugged. "A girl I used to know."

She didn't say any more.

"How did it happen, Mom?" Catherine said. "I mean, how was he . . . ?" She hesitated, reluctant to say "murdered." It was such an ugly word. How could her own mother be involved in something like that? Finally she changed it to, "How did he die?"

Her mother leaned back against the sofa cushions. "I thought I'd never have to think about this again, but I guess you need to know." She took another deep breath. "Joe Sims and I grew up together. We dated as soon as we were old enough. To me it was just friendly, like going out with my brother. But Joe thought we were steadies, or whatever it is you call it nowadays." She stopped, and her eyes seemed to gaze into the past.

"Go on, Mom," Catherine prompted.

"Then I met Travis. T.J."

She stopped for a moment, then went on. "T.J. and I liked each other immediately. One of those 'like at first sight' things."

Travis glanced at Catherine and smiled a little as if to say that had happened to him, too.

"T.J. and I started going out together a lot, which left little time for Joe. I thought he was handling it okay, but then he started doing odd things. He'd camp outside my house. He'd watch me. He'd follow T.J. and me around." She stopped again.

Catherine and Travis waited.

Her mother put her hand over her eyes. "I should have done something."

"What?" Travis asked softly.

She shook her head. "I don't know. I should have broken off with T.J. or something."

"And let Joe ruin your life?" Catherine asked.

Her mother sat up straight, removing her hand from her eyes. "Then T.J. would still be alive," she said. "He'd have had a chance to grow up and have a family." Her face was twisted with misery.

Catherine put her arms around her. "You don't have to say any more if you don't want to, Mom. This is too hard."

Her mother shook her head. "No. I want to tell you." She rubbed a hand across her face. "T.J. and I came home late from a school dance one night. Joe had been there on the sidelines, watching. He followed us home. He got out of his car and came over to T.J.'s car."

"And shot him?" Catherine said when she stopped again.

"Not before I told him to get out of my life," her mother said. "I told him I valued him as a friend, but I wasn't his girl and that I didn't want to go out with him any more. That's when he pulled the gun from his pocket. It was all my fault. If I hadn't yelled at him, maybe he wouldn't have shot T.J."

The three of them sat there for a long time after she finished telling the story.

Then Catherine's mother reached out for

the box of tissues on the lamp table. She blew her nose, drew a deep, quivery breath, then smiled at Travis. "Well, Travis," she said, "has our town lived up to your expectations?"

He seemed startled by her abrupt change of subject. "Yes," he said. He looked at Catherine. "I really like it here, Mrs. Belmont."

"Good." Catherine's mother got to her feet. "I'll leave you to sort out all I've told you. And Travis, tell your mother I said. . . ." She made a scrubbing motion with her hand. "No. Don't tell her anything. She wouldn't want to hear anything from me."

She went to her room.

"Cathy," Travis said as soon as the door closed. "Aren't you going to tell her about today? About what happened in the auditorium?"

Catherine shook her head. "She has enough on her mind right now. I don't want her worrying about that, especially after what she told us tonight."

"But you're going to tell her later," Travis said.

When Catherine didn't say anything, he said, "I'll go with you to Andersen's tomorrow to watch *Lost River*. We'll see what kind of funny ideas somebody might get for the next little terror session."

Catherine wondered if she even wanted to see the soap the next day.

Before she could decide one way or another, he said, "You can trust me, Cathy."

"Okay," she said finally.

After Travis left, Catherine knocked on her mother's bedroom door. "Are you all right, Mom?"

"I'm fine." She didn't invite Catherine in to talk.

"Good night, Mom," Catherine said. "I love you."

"Love you, too, honey. Good night."

The phone rang.

"If that's somebody for me, tell them I'll call back tomorrow," Catherine's mother said.

It wasn't for her. It was Liz.

"Cath," she said. "Is Travis gone?"

"Yes. Why?"

"Did he do anything?" Liz asked. "I mean did he flip out or anything like that?"

"Flip out? What are you talking about, Liz."

"Travis," Liz said. "*You* know."

Catherine felt a little sick to her stomach. "No, I *don't* know. Tell me."

"Britny said she *told* you about Travis." Liz's voice was urgent. "You'd better watch him carefully."

Catherine didn't say anything. She *couldn't* say anything.

"Cath." Liz sounded sympathetic now. "Travis Cavanaugh is a nut case."

Chapter 12

"Liz," Catherine gasped. "How can you say a thing like that?"

"It's true, Cath. I'm sorry." Liz's voice was gentle and sympathetic. "Britny told me, and she should know."

Catherine tried to gather her wits together. "Since when are you chummy with Britny?"

"I'm not. But she's been worried about him. And you. She told me because I'm your friend."

"Goody for Britny," Catherine said. "Did it ever occur to you that she's just trying to scare me away from him?"

"Why don't you ask Travis? He mentioned being laid up last summer with a broken leg, that day at Andersen's when we first met him. Remember?"

"I remember."

"There was more to it."

Catherine waited.

"It was a Rollerblade accident."

"I know that."

"Did you know he smacked into another guy and really hurt him? The guy is paralyzed because of Travis. Permanently. It made Travis crazy. He started doing weird things after his leg healed."

"What kind of weird things?" Catherine asked.

"Britny told me he'd draw pictures of tombstones with people's names on them," Liz said. "He'd kind of slink around and scare people. Seemed to want to get himself put away somewhere or something. I don't know what else. Ask him. No, on second thought, don't ask him. You can never tell what he might do."

"He can't be dangerous." Catherine tried to sound sure, but her voice trembled as she spoke.

There was a pause before Liz replied. "Look, I'm sorry that I didn't break the news a little better. I really thought you knew. I thought you might be trying to help him or something and I was worried about your being alone with him."

"Is that why you and Kade followed us to the restaurant?"

"Yes," Liz said.

"How did you know where we were?"

"Kade knew. He watches you, you know." Liz's voice changed, became brisk and businesslike. "Listen, just keep your door locked. I'm sure your mother is home by now. Try to get some sleep. I'll see you tomorrow."

After Liz hung up, Catherine sat for a long time trying to make sense out of what she'd just learned. But there was no sense in it. If Travis was dangerous, she would have noticed something odd by now, wouldn't she?

How about the Whisperer in the auditorium? That was odd enough, wasn't it? Travis could very well have been the Whisperer, despite what he said.

That thought was in her mind when she heard a soft rap at the door.

She jumped to her feet and stood rigid, listening. Had it been her imagination?

There were night sounds outside. Crickets. A car passing. Maybe Old Albert had been thumping around downstairs.

No. There it was again. A soft tap, tap, tap at the door. Then it came again, this time a little louder. TAP, TAP, TAP.

"Cath," someone said in a loud whisper. "Open the door."

Was that the same whisper she'd heard in the auditorium?

"Cath." Now the person spoke aloud. "Are you all right? Open up."

It was Kade.

Relief made Catherine weak. She ran to the door and opened it.

"Kade," she said. She wondered what he'd do if she hugged him.

"I was about to bust in," Kade said, coming inside.

She closed the door, making sure it was locked. "Bust in? Why?"

He looked over her shoulder into the apartment. "Well, Travis Cavanaugh's car was out in front for a long time. I was worried about you."

Catherine's legs felt rubbery and she motioned Kade toward the sofa so she could sit. "So you know about Travis."

"Liz told me. And after that weird stuff in the auditorium, I just wanted to keep an eye on you."

She hadn't told Kade anything about that. "Who told you about the auditorium?"

"Liz," Kade said. "She said the lights went out while you were there."

"Just like the lights went out on Cassandra in today's episode of *Lost River*," Catherine said.

There was that look again, that slightly disbelieving look. That look that said Kade thought Catherine was losing reality. He wiped it away quickly and said, "I'll watch over you, Cath. I can see you here in the living room from my window. I'll be watching."

Suddenly Catherine's heart began thudding. She remembered what her mother had said about Joe Sims. *He watched me,* she'd said. *He was always watching me.*

"Kade, I have to do some homework before I go to bed," Catherine said. "You don't have to watch me. I'll be all right."

"Do you want me to go?" Kade sounded bewildered.

Catherine nodded. "I'll see you in the morning." Morning, when the shadows were gone and the sun was bright.

"Okay." He got up and walked to the door. "Let me know if you need me." He started down the stairs. "I *like* watching you, Cath," he said back over his shoulder.

After she closed the door and put the chain on it, Catherine hurried over and pulled down the shades on the windows that faced Kade's house. She tried to keep her mind away from the thought of his watching her. Watching and following her.

He had known where she and Travis were going for dinner.

Her hands shaking, she felt around the telephone, along the underside of the little table on which it sat, around the lampshade, searching for an electronic bug.

It was useless. These were the places Kade and Liz had looked for the bug the day of the strange telephone call. If he'd planted a bug, he'd have put it in a less obvious place.

But how could she suspect Kade? He was her friend.

Joe Sims had been her mother's friend.

Something suddenly hit Catherine. Kade had said Liz told him about the auditorium incident.

But Liz didn't know. Catherine hadn't said anything about it to Liz.

It took her a long time to go to sleep that night, and when she did her dreams were frightening. There was darkness and voices. Britny was there, and Kade, then Catherine was going over a cliff in somebody's car. Down, down, down, like Cassandra had done, and she had screamed.

Her mother called out, asking if she was all right.

"Nightmares," Catherine called back.

"Want me to come in?" Mom asked.

"No." Why make both of them lose sleep? "I'll be all right now, Mom."

She knew she wasn't going to sleep any more. She didn't really want to close her eyes, but somewhere near dawn she did.

She woke feeling dull and tired. She looked in her closet for something that *wouldn't* look like Cassandra. But most of her clothing had been selected reflecting Cassandra's taste.

Finally she pulled out a pair of black pants and a gold shirt like Cassandra had worn way back when she went with Dane Ransom, before Weston Fremont. That was when she'd still had long hair, so it didn't seem so much like Catherine was copying her.

Liz was waiting in the driveway when she went downstairs to go to school.

"Hi," Liz said. "You look as if you had a bad night." Her face was concerned.

Catherine nodded. "Did you say something to Kade about what happened yesterday in the auditorium?"

Liz put her hand over her mouth. "Wasn't I supposed to? Was it a secret?"

"I just wondered how *you* knew about it. I didn't tell you."

"Britny told me. When she was telling me about Travis's problem."

"How did Britny know?"

"Gosh Cath, I don't know." Liz sounded annoyed. "You're getting nutsier and nutsier."

"I'm sorry." Catherine's head ached. She couldn't keep track of who told whom what. "I didn't mean to beat you over the head, Liz," she said. "I just don't know what's going on."

"I'll help if I can," Liz said.

"I know." Catherine wasn't sure Liz *could* help. What was there to do?

There was one thing. But it was something she had to do herself. She could find out who had keys to the sound room. She knew there was a limited number of keys given out each year. Only certain qualified people were allowed to have one.

She didn't mention it to Liz. They talked about their English class and the weather and clothes the rest of the way to school.

When they got there, Catherine told Liz she'd be a little late to class.

"Just want to check on something in the office," she said. "Tell Mr. Gormley I'll be there soon."

After Liz disappeared up the stairs, she went to the office. The information she needed would be there.

She smiled at Mrs. Simonsen, the principal's

secretary, then looked at the bulletin board where information on various committees was posted.

The list of people she wanted wasn't where it usually was.

"I'd like to see the list of people who have sound room keys," she said to Mrs. Simonsen. "It's not here on the board."

"No? It *should* be there," Mrs. Simonsen said. "I saw it a couple days ago." She shuffled through a stack of papers on her desk. "It must be here somewhere." She gave up on the stack and opened a file drawer. "I need a secretary myself," she muttered as she flipped through the files. "Never have time to get things organized." She looked up. "Is it important?"

"Yes," Catherine said.

"Why do you need it?" Mrs. Simonsen shuffled through the stack of papers as she spoke.

"Erin and Suzanne and I are supposed to do a routine for the next assembly," Catherine said smoothly. "I need to contact somebody about lights and stuff." That was true enough, but not quite the whole truth.

"So many kids coming through here all the time," Mrs. S. grumbled. "I guess somebody borrowed the list and forgot to put it back on the board."

Or maybe somebody destroyed it. Somebody who didn't want anybody to remember who had keys.

Finally Mrs. Simonsen looked up helplessly. "It just isn't here, Catherine. Sorry."

"Thanks anyway, Mrs. S." Her face must have shown her disappointment because Mrs. Simonsen picked up her telephone.

"Wait," she said. "Let me call Mr. Drucker. He always remembers everything."

Mr. Drucker was the principal. Catherine waited as Mrs. S. pushed a buzzer and explained what she wanted. She scribbled names as she listened to what Mr. Drucker said, then looked up at Catherine with a smile.

"Here they are." She thumped the paper in front of her. "The people who have keys to the sound room are Ikey Brotman, Sharon Hurst, Blair Colby, and that new boy. Have you met him yet? His name is Travis Cavanaugh."

Chapter 13

Catherine had to force herself not to put her hands over her ears. If Travis was the Whisperer, she didn't want to hear about it. She couldn't keep on doing this seesawing, this coming to trust somebody then finding out that person was not to be trusted.

"Is something wrong?" Mrs. Simonsen asked, her brown eyes worried. "Are you all right, Catherine?" She got up from her chair. "Here, sit down." She tugged gently at Catherine's arm, guiding her to the chair.

"I'm okay." Catherine pulled away. "Are you sure Mr. Drucker said 'Travis Cavanaugh?' Could you have heard wrong?"

"No, Catherine. Besides, I remember that his name was on the list of people authorized to operate the sound room. It stuck in my mind because he's new." Mrs. Simonsen peered into Catherine's face. "Let me get you a glass of water."

"No. No. I have to go." Catherine clutched her books and hurried from the office. There was no question of going to class. She couldn't concentrate. She couldn't even think, except to remember Travis's kind face the night before as he said, "You can trust me."

Hugging her books to her chest, she ran awkwardly down the empty corridor, past the auditorium doors and the glass-fronted cases where the athletic trophies were displayed. She caught sight of herself in the mirrors in back of the trophies. She would have sworn it was Cassandra dashing down the corridor, even though Cassandra didn't wear things like the gold shirt and black pants anymore. She still looked like Cassandra, small and slender with short, dark hair.

Was Cassandra running, too? Had she gotten out of the dark auditorium filled with the scent of roses?

No, that was Catherine's own life where that had happened. Cassandra was in her bedroom, waiting for Dr. Wyatt to come back with the hot milk. But the lights had gone out and the whispering had begun. And there was the scent of roses.

Shaking now, Catherine continued running,

turning her eyes away from the mirrors and looking instead at the rows of graffiti-decorated lockers on the other side of the corridor. It wouldn't have surprised her if one of the locker doors had swung open and something hideous had sprung out. What new tortures did Travis have in mind for her?

She turned a corner, heading for one of the back doors of the building. She would go home. Her mother would still be there. She didn't leave for work until after noon. Catherine would tell her everything, and together they would figure out what to do.

No. What if Travis was outside of her house, waiting for her? Or would Kade be out there, watching, watching, watching?

Or Dr. Carlton Wyatt?

What was reality and what was fantasy?

Panting with terror, Catherine whirled to run back to the office where it was safe. But she ran smack into Travis.

Something fell to the floor as they collided, something that hit the concrete floor with a metallic jangle. A knife maybe?

She looked down. Keys. Travis's key ring.

Catherine's air was knocked out of her and she couldn't even scream.

"Cathy," Travis exclaimed. "I was looking for you." He reached out both hands and took hold of her upper arms. "Hey, you're trembling. What's the matter?"

She backed away from him, holding her books out in front as if to fend him off. "Stay away!" she said. "Don't touch me."

He jerked his hands away as if she were on fire. "What's happened, Cathy?" He looked up and down the corridor as if that would give him the answer.

She continued backing away. "I know that you have one of the four keys to the sound room, Travis. You were the Whisperer in the auditorium."

Her voice echoed down the corridor, sounding hollow like Cassandra's did the time she'd had a nervous breakdown and everything went a little out of focus. Catherine felt that way now. She felt like Cassandra.

She stood poised to run if Travis moved toward her.

He didn't move at all. He didn't speak for half a minute. Then he said softly, "Is that what you believe, Cathy? Why not Blair, or Sharon, or Ikey? They all have keys, too."

"Because you were here after school yesterday." Catherine couldn't control her wobbly voice. "You knew where I was going and who was supposed to be there with me."

He didn't say anything.

What was he thinking? What was he going to do?

Travis didn't do anything. He just stood there gazing sadly at her. The only move he made was to bend down and pick up his key ring from the floor.

"Cathy," he said softly. "I went to your classroom, but you weren't there. Liz said you'd gone to the office, so I was checking that out. I wanted to ask you to go with me to the sound room to see if we could pick up any clues about who was there yesterday."

"Is that truly what you wanted me for?" Catherine scrubbed her hand across her face. The feeling of unreality persisted. She felt as if she were saying lines that had been written for her. Was this real?

"Yes," Travis said. "That truly is what I wanted you for. If you're afraid of me, then go to the sound room alone. Here, I'll let you take my key, even if that's against the rules."

He fingered through the ring of keys, then went quickly through them all again. "It's not here," he said in a voice gone suddenly hoarse.

What kind of game was he playing?

He raised his eyes to Catherine's. "I've lost the key to the sound room," he whispered. "But how could it slip off my ring?"

He held the ring out to her. Without touching it, she saw that it was a thick, sturdy ring and it was unlikely that a key could just fall off.

"Somebody must have *taken* it off," he said.

Catherine thought about running to the office while he was concentrating on the keys. But he looked so tragic that her doubts began to fade again.

"Who could have taken the key?" she said. "Who had the opportunity? Is your key ring ever out of your sight?"

He shook his head slowly. "Never. Except during gym class when it's inside my locker." He seemed to be thinking. "But there was no sign that my locker had been broken into."

Catherine heard a burst of laughter from a nearby classroom. It added to her sense of unreality. Where were the TV cameras? When was this scene going to end?

She had to get out of here, away from Travis. She didn't care to know the next line of this script.

She started to move slowly toward the office, but before she could take more than four steps, Travis said, "Wait a minute!"

She thought he was speaking to her, and she began to run.

"Wait a minute!" he said again. "Cathy, come back. I just thought of something."

She stopped but didn't return to him. Instead, he walked slowly toward her as he spoke. She felt mesmerized, frozen in mid-action.

"There was another time the keys were out of my sight," Travis said. "Yesterday, Mr. Cameron sent me and . . . uh . . . sent a couple of us from my electronics class uptown to get something. We went in my car, and she . . . the other person . . . was listening to music on the radio. She wanted to hear the end of a song, so I left my keys in the car while I went into the store. She came in a little later."

"She?" Catherine said. "Who was with you?"

He shook his head miserably, saying nothing.

"Tell me, Travis. This is important."

She didn't think he was going to tell her, but finally he blurted, "Britny. She was with me."

Catherine felt as if a cold wind had just swept down the corridor. "Britny took the key from your ring."

It made sense. Britny had always hated Catherine. She must hate her even more now that Travis liked her.

Britny could have edited that tape together. She was in the class that Kade and Travis took.

Travis stared down the corridor. "We have to find out which class she has this period. Maybe she'll tell me if she has the key." He started walking toward the office. Catherine followed.

The only thing they found out at the office was that Britny was not at school that day. Mrs. Simonsen said she'd phoned in that morning, saying she had to go somewhere with her parents.

Or maybe she'd just stayed home to watch *Lost River* and decide what was to come next in the script she was preparing for Catherine. Try as she might, Catherine couldn't keep that thought from her mind as she and Travis left the office.

"Think I ought to report my key missing?" Travis asked.

"Not yet," Catherine said. "Let's see if we can get in touch with Britny first."

Even as she said it, Catherine realized the hopelessness of finding out anything from Britny. Would Britny meekly admit she took the key, a big offense in itself, and then rattle off all the things she'd done to Catherine? No way.

Britny wasn't home when Travis tried to call her from the pay phone by the gym. Or at least she didn't answer, and neither did anybody else.

"I'll go over to her house after school." Travis's face was troubled. "We might as well just go to classes for the rest of the day."

After thinking about it, Catherine agreed. She was probably as safe there at school as she was anywhere else. No use worrying Mom yet.

But she still didn't want to watch that day's episode of *Lost River*. She hadn't set her VCR that morning to tape it, and when Travis reminded her that they were going to walk uptown at lunchtime to see it, she said she didn't want to.

She told Liz the same thing a little later.

"I don't want to see it today," she said without offering an explanation. There was no explanation, except that she was afraid of sliding into Cassandra that day. Cassandra, who was in danger.

"Because of the auditorium thing?" Liz asked.

Catherine nodded.

"Well," Liz said, "if you really think somebody is getting ideas from it to do more things to you, maybe you should be prepared."

Maybe she should. "You go watch it, will you, Liz? You can tell me what happens if there's anything I should know."

"I'll do it." Liz's face was full of sympathy.

Maybe she was finally realizing that Catherine was telling the truth about the things that had been happening.

Their English class after lunch had already started when Liz got back from Andersen's. She came tiptoeing in and slipped into the desk behind Catherine.

"Cath." She leaned forward, trying to avoid the eyes of Mrs. Olsen who was talking about verbs. "You won't believe what happened."

Mrs. Olsen glared at her. "Elizabeth," she said, "it's rude enough to disrupt us by coming in late, without whispering to your neighbor. If you have something to say, perhaps we should all hear."

Liz sat up straight. "Sorry," she muttered.

As Mrs. Olsen went on lecturing, Catherine heard Liz open her notebook. There was the soft scratch of a pencil on paper, and when the teacher turned her back to write on the chalk-board, Liz shoved a note into Catherine's hand.

Carefully, Catherine unfolded the scrap of paper, dreading to see what Liz had to tell.

SOMEBODY'S KIDNAPPING CASSAN-DRA, Liz's big, bold handwriting told her. WHOEVER IT IS CAME INTO HER BED-ROOM AFTER THE LIGHTS WENT OUT AND THREW A BLACK BAG OVER HER HEAD. HE DRAGGED HER INTO A CAR. I DON'T KNOW WHO IT IS BECAUSE ALL IT SHOWED WAS A PERSON IN A LONG BLACK COAT WITH A HOOD.

The hooded figure again!

It didn't take much thinking to figure out where Britny was that day. She was out shop-ping for a long black coat with a hood.

Hardly realizing what she was doing, Cath-erine leapt to her feet, scattering her books on the floor. As she ran from the room she heard someone snicker and say, "Must be soap time."

Liz called out to her, but she didn't stop. Footsteps pounded down the corridor behind her, but she kept on going. She had a good head start and was able to lose herself behind the gym before anyone could catch up with her. She ran toward Jepsen Park where she dodged behind one bush and then another so no one could follow her.

She knew she wasn't being rational about this, but she had to get home. It seemed like the only safe place.

She ran all the way to her house, pounding up the stairs to her apartment.

"Stop that noise," Old Albert screeched.

Why didn't he come out and see why she was home in the middle of the day? Why didn't he care?

Catherine's mother had already gone to work, and the door was locked. Catherine held the screen door open with her foot while she fumbled in her pants pocket for her key and fitted it into the lock.

Then she was afraid to go inside. She wished somebody would come now and be with her. Kade. Travis. Liz. Anybody but Britny.

She entered the apartment slowly, letting her eyes adjust to the dimness of the living room. There were no bloodred roses waiting for her on the table, nor on top of the TV. There was no dark-coated person lurking in the shadows of the hallway.

Breathing a little easier, Catherine slammed the door shut and put on the chain. She was now a little embarrassed that she'd fled from the classroom the way she did. The other kids would rag her à lot about that.

Hurrying across the living room, she went into her mother's bedroom. It was full of the familiar things she'd known since she was a baby. It was always comforting, being there.

Catherine sat down on the bed and looked around for something to take her mind off Britny. She picked up the photo album that still lay on the bedside table. She turned the pages, avoiding the one with the big picture of Travis Jalinsky.

Talking softly to herself, she looked instead at the happy pictures, the ones filled with laughing girls or guys showing off their biceps. T. J. was in a lot of the pictures. "T. J., who died," she said.

Catherine put the album down at the same time that she heard a car turning into the driveway.

She ran to the living room and looked out of the window to the driveway. The car had gone past the stairs and all she could see was its rear bumper.

Cautiously she went to the door and opened it a crack. No one was out there.

Opening the door wider, Catherine pushed at the screen door and stepped out onto the little balcony to see who was in the driveway.

Before she could go out far enough to see whose car had driven in, someone rammed the screen door against her, knocking her down. He must have been standing behind the potted ficus tree, hidden by its thick leaves.

Catherine glimpsed a figure in a long, hooded coat.

Then something heavy and stifling and dark was yanked down over her head.

Chapter 14

Catherine struggled to free herself from the smothering folds of thick cloth that seemed to go down almost as far as her knees. But strong arms circled her and held her firmly. She couldn't scream because one of the arms was locked around her head, pressing the heavy material against her mouth so that she could scarcely breathe.

In desperation she drummed her heels on the porch, hoping that Old Albert would come running out of his house in fury to see what was going on.

But nobody came.

"No use, Catherine," a whispery voice said in her ear. "Nobody's going to hear you."

It sounded like the same voice that had come over the loudspeaker system in the auditorium. She couldn't be sure, but it had the same feathery quality to it.

She wanted to scream at her captor, ask why he was doing this to her. What had she done to him? What made him want to hurt her?

And above all, who was he?

Pinned as she was by the strong arms, Catherine could only submit to being dragged down the stairs.

She could scarcely breathe inside the stifling bag. Her heart lurched and stopped from fright, then started up again, whacking against her ribs so loud she was sure Old Albert must hear it. Why didn't he yell about the noise? Why didn't he come out to see what was happening?

In her terror, Catherine could barely think. But a flash of memory replayed Liz's note about that day's episode of *Lost River*. The hooded figure had put Cassandra in a car and was speeding off somewhere with her. Cassandra didn't know who her captor was, any more than Catherine knew who was abducting her.

So was the Whisperer following the script exactly? How would he know what to do when they got wherever he was taking her? How did he know where to take her? Did he have some way of knowing what would happen on the show tomorrow?

When they got to the bottom of the stairs,

Catherine was pushed inside a car. The Whisperer must have left the door open when he came up the stairs so he wouldn't have to let go of her long enough to reach for the handle.

He shoved her onto the seat, and before she had a chance to try to free herself she felt a rope being wrapped around her, binding her arms to her sides.

Now that his arm was no longer choking her, Catherine screamed, but her captor quickly replaced his arm, choking off her air.

"Don't do that," he whispered. "It could be fatal."

Catherine shut off the screams. Nobody was around to hear anyway.

"Why are you doing this?" she demanded as soon as her kidnapper removed his arm again.

The Whisperer didn't answer. He slammed the car door.

Catherine was uncomfortable, pushed down on the seat as she was. She struggled to sit upright, her arms clamped to her sides by the ropes. That was better, but she could barely suck in any air through the thick folds of the bag over her upper body.

The driver's side door opened. Catherine felt the car bounce a little as the Whisperer got in behind the steering wheel. He seemed to be right beside her, so she figured she was in the passenger side of the front seat.

Oh, why, why didn't Old Albert come out to see what was going on?

Was Old Albert the Whisperer? Or was he just off on one of his infrequent trips to the grocery store?

Terror choked Catherine as tightly as the arms had done a few minutes before. Terror and the heavy bag.

"I can't breathe," she gasped.

The Whisperer chuckled, a dry, rattly sound deep in his throat.

Catherine felt him lean across her, heard him open the glove compartment, then there were tiny snicking sounds. He was using a scissors to cut a small hole in the heavy bag, near her nose.

"Thank you," she said sincerely as she felt a tiny rush of oxygen.

The Whisperer started the motor and backed out of the driveway, then sped off down the street. To the left, as near as Catherine could tell. So they weren't going to the school. That was the other way.

Where then?

Catherine felt dizzy as the car squealed around corners and screeched to jolting stops at signals. Catherine knew only one person who drove like that. Kade.

"Kade?" she said.

He didn't answer.

This was unreal. Was it actually happening, or had she slipped totally into the soap opera? Her stomach lurched.

"I'm sick," she said. "I'm going to barf."

"Your problem." The Whisperer's raspy voice was unsympathetic.

Catherine tried to concentrate on something else. The sound of the engine. Did it *sound* like Kade's car? Britny's? Travis's?

She couldn't tell anything from the car's noises.

If only she could figure out who the Whisperer was. It might help her to know how to plead with him. He was bigger than she was. That much she knew. Too big to be a girl, so that ruled out Britny. It had to be Kade. Or Travis.

The air hole! Maybe she could see enough through the air hole to identify the Whisperer.

The hole was near her nose. By turning her eyes downward, she could see light. Perhaps if she tipped her head up, she could see the Whisperer's face.

She tried it. But no matter how she twisted

her head, she couldn't see far enough up to get a glimpse of his face.

What she could see was a dark blue coat or robe of some sort. Thick and bulky, like a winter coat. He must be as hot in that as she was in the heavy bag.

Kade didn't have a blue winter coat as far as she knew. Certainly not one with a hood.

Her heart hammered again as she thought of that hood. The hooded figure from *Lost River*. The one who meant to harm Cassandra. The one who left the bloodred roses.

Who had kidnapped Cassandra?

Who had kidnapped *her*?

Maybe she could get a clue from his shoes. But she couldn't get a glimpse of them, either. They were hidden by the way the coat was draped over the edge of the seat.

Catherine's arms were beginning to hurt. The binding cords were too tight, and she felt as if her circulation was being cut off. Her fingers tingled.

She shifted on the car seat as much as she could, trying to relieve the pressure.

"Settle down," the Whisperer said, "or I'll add more ropes."

Catherine didn't want that. She eased back against the seat.

Now she could see the gearshift through the air hole in the bag.

The gearshift!

She knew that gearshift. She'd noticed it the day Travis drove her home from school. The carved head of a dog. The one Travis had made while his injured leg mended.

Oh, no! Travis was the Whisperer. Travis, whom she'd decided to trust. Travis, who according to Liz, was a nut case.

It made sense. He was getting even for what had happened to his uncle T.J. His mother had probably talked about it all his life. Travis was getting revenge.

She felt sicker than ever.

"Travis," she said. "Where are you taking me?"

There was a moment of silence, then another of those dry chuckles.

"You can talk now," Catherine told him. "Now that I know who you are."

Silence.

Strangely enough, Catherine felt calmer now that she'd identified the Whisperer. Probably Travis had been planning this ever since that day at Andersen's Appliances when he'd come up to talk to her. He must have already known who she was. Her mother had been

171

right about his reasons for getting acquainted with her.

"Where are you taking me?" she repeated. "What are you going to do to me?"

There was that dry chuckle again, then Travis whispered, "We'll find out tomorrow."

So that's what he had in mind. They'd watch tomorrow's show, then he'd carry out whatever happened to Cassandra.

But soap opera people didn't die, did they?

Yes, they did. Catherine knew of several. And Britny had said the producers of the show might kill off Cassandra's character so the actress could go on to do something else. Had Travis got the idea from Britny?

It had been a while since there'd been a murder on *Lost River*. Murders always made good plot twists because there was a lot of suspense and they could spend weeks figuring out who the murderer was. Then there were the courtroom trial scenes.

Yes, soap opera people *did* die.

Catherine felt smothered again, more by her thoughts than by the bag. What was she going to do?

They rode along silently for what Catherine guessed was about half an hour. Then she felt the car turn off the main highway and bump along a lengthy stretch of rutted road.

It stopped.

"Don't try anything funny or I'll tie you down so you can't move," Travis whispered.

What could she do? Her arms were firmly bound down, and it would be hard to try to kick him since she couldn't see.

Travis got out and came around to her side of the car. He opened the door, then helped her to stand up.

"I'll get behind you and guide you by the shoulders," he whispered. "Just walk where I point you."

What else could she do? She did as he said, listening for identifying sounds, like wind in trees or waves crashing on the beach or the rush of traffic, just so she would know where they were. But through the heavy material over her head she could hear nothing but their feet crunching on gravel as they walked.

"Stop," Travis whispered after they had climbed three steps to what must have been a porch.

Catherine heard the jingle of keys, then the opening of a door. Travis guided her into a room and closed the door.

Positioning her against something solid, Travis loosened the ropes around her body just enough so he could reach under the heavy bag and grab her hands. Pulling them behind her, he tied them to whatever she was leaning against, some kind of post.

"How about taking me out of this bag now?" she asked. "Even with the breathing hole you cut for me, I'm not getting enough air."

"That's one of the things I like about you, Cathy," he whispered. "You've got a lot of spirit."

Nobody but Travis called her Cathy.

"How do you know anything about me?" she said. "You've barely known me long enough to get acquainted."

Travis laughed, that whispery, dry sound that she hated.

"So how about it?" she asked. "Are you going to let me out of this bag? At least let me see where I'll be spending my last moments."

"All right." His whispering voice became firm and threatening. "But no funny stuff. I'm going to tie your feet before I do anything else."

She could feel him wrapping a rope around her ankles, then around the post. He worked silently.

"Travis," she said, "why don't you tell me now why you're doing this? I can't get away. Is it because of what happened to your uncle? I had nothing to do with that."

Silence.

He started to pull at the stifling bag. He did it slowly, as if to tease her.

The bag was almost off. At last Catherine could breathe real air again, not just snatches of oxygen filtered through the small breathing hole.

She drew in a deep breath as he pulled the bag all the way off and let it drop to the floor.

Catherine raised her eyes to look at him, then gasped in disbelief.

It wasn't Travis standing there before her.

It wasn't Travis at all.

Chapter 15

"Liz!" Catherine gasped.

It was Liz, in a thick blue coat with a hood.

Liz smiled. "Surprised, Cath?"

Catherine stared at her. This wasn't possible. It had to be a joke.

But Liz's smile was cold and cruel.

"Liz," Catherine choked. "Why?"

"Why what? Isn't this just like something that would happen on *Lost River?* You've been living in that show for a long time, Cath. This is just the latest episode."

Liz took off the big coat, and a thick sweater she'd had underneath it. No wonder she had seemed as big as Travis or Kade. She'd padded herself so she'd feel bigger to Catherine.

She continued to smile. There was no humor in it, no warmth. It was a hard, mocking smile. Catherine had never seen anything like that on Liz's face before. It made her heart wham against her ribs.

"Liz." She had to try again. "Liz, listen to me. Maybe I *was* obsessed with *Lost River*. But what does that have to do with you and me? We've been friends for a long time. You've *got* to tell me why you're doing this."

"Shut up, Cath!" Liz came to stand right in front of her, and for a moment Catherine thought Liz was going to slap her.

She didn't say anything more.

Liz's eyes were wild and staring. She seemed capable of anything.

She stood there glaring at Catherine for what seemed like an hour. Finally she turned and walked over to look out of the window. "Just keep quiet," she said over her shoulder. "Let me think."

Catherine leaned back against the post and looked around the room. Where were they? It seemed to be a secluded cabin. They were in a fairly large room, with a fireplace in the opposite wall.

Behind her was a rough lumber stairway leading up. The post to which she was tied was the anchor for the stair railing.

Catherine twisted her hands so her fingers could explore the knots in the ropes around her wrists. Her hands were so sweaty with fright that she thought they might slip right out of the ropes. But the knots were tight and solid.

Wait. She could feel something there on the post that pressed into her back. A nail. Probably something left over from attaching Christmas decorations to the stair rail, or something like that.

She could feel the nail head, flat and cold. If only she could hook the knots over that nail, she might be able to work them loose.

But the knots were too solid even for that.

Taking a deep breath so her voice wouldn't quiver, Catherine said, "Liz, the ropes are too tight. They're shutting off the circulation in my hands. Could you adjust them just a little?"

Liz was not dumb. "Sure," she said, turning her head. "And pretty soon you'd work yourself free. Forget it, Cath. I left enough slack so your blood can get through."

She smiled a little when she said "blood."

"It doesn't matter much anyhow, in the long run." She left the window and went to sit on the sofa, staring at the floor as if she were thinking.

There was no use trying to get her to loosen the ropes. Catherine glanced around for other possibilities. What could she do? What might be of use to her? What was available there in the cabin?

There were the usual tools in a little stand beside the fireplace. A poker. A small shovel. A little broom. If she could get hold of that poker, she'd have a weapon. But how could she get across the room?

There wasn't much furniture. There was the sofa on which Liz sat. There were some chairs by the low kitchen counter in one corner. Near Catherine was a spindly little long-legged table, just big enough for the black telephone that sat on top of it.

If only she could get to that telephone she could call Travis. Or Kade. Or the police. Or someone.

But it was a dial phone, and even if she could reach it Liz would be sure to hear her dialing.

Catherine wondered if she could kick over the table and knock the phone to the floor. But what good would that do?

With her eyes she measured the distance to the table. Too far to reach.

She continued to examine her surroundings. The windows in the room were large, floor to ceiling, and they looked out on tall pines with mountains in the background. She could see the glimmer of blue water through the pines.

A cabin in the mountains. That's where they were.

Catherine cleared her throat, and trying for a calm voice she said, "I didn't know your uncle's family had a cabin, Liz. This is nice." If she could draw Liz into a simple conversation, perhaps she could reason with her.

Liz nodded. "It's not my uncle's. It belongs to Travis's and Britny's families."

Catherine remembered the day Britny had given Travis the key to the cabin. "You must have been watching the day Britny gave that key to Travis and he put it on his ring."

"Yes," Liz said. "I'm tricky with keys." She laughed. "I took the key to the sound room from right under Britny's nose. I was uptown and saw her sitting in Travis's car while he went into a store to get something. I guess she stayed out to listen to the radio. I got in and chatted with her and took off the key while that ninny snapped her fingers and closed her eyes and floated along on the music."

"What were you doing uptown?" Catherine asked in an effort to keep her talking. "That was during school hours."

"I sneaked away from study hall," Liz said. "I wanted to buy a screwdriver or something so I could break into the sound room. I knew you were going to be in the auditorium after school. After I got Travis's key, I didn't need the screwdriver anymore."

Catherine swallowed. Her voice kept wanting to wobble out of control. "It was Travis's car we came here in," she said. "You knew the cabin key was on his ring and that's why we came here." She didn't wait for Liz to confirm or deny that, nor did she ask how Liz got Travis's car. "How long have you been planning all this?" she asked.

Liz laughed. "Since Travis said how much you look like Cassandra. Actually, before that, but that's when I decided *how* to do it. My mother has kept track of your family all these years. So I made sure I got acquainted with you when I moved to Greenville to live with my aunt. I've been waiting for a long time."

"Your mother?" Catherine was more bewildered than ever. "What does your mother have to do with my family?" She thought about it. "Are you related to T. J. Jalinsky, too?"

"T. J. wasn't the only one whose life was ruined by your mother," Liz said. "Joe Sims was my mother's brother. He's been in a psycho ward ever since your mother made him shoot T. J. Jalinsky."

Catherine gasped. Joe Sims. Liz was related to the guy who'd killed Travis's uncle T. J.

"They're twins, my mother and Uncle Joe," Liz went on, almost as if speaking to herself. "His life was ruined, and hers, too. She got married and had me, but the marriage didn't work out. She was too upset about her twin brother being locked up for the rest of his life. It made her sick, too. She's in the same place as he is now."

"You mean in a psycho ward?" Catherine wondered if she should have asked that, but it was said now.

Liz didn't react. She merely said, "Yes. A psycho ward. Where they keep insane people." She stood up. "Can you imagine, Cath, how it is to think of your own mother in a psycho ward? To lose her when you're just a little kid, and grow up without her?"

"It's been hard for you," Catherine said gently, trying to calm Liz. "I'm sorry."

"You should be." Liz sat down on the sofa again.

Catherine cleared her throat. "Is her name Tessa?" she asked. "Your mother?" She remembered her own mother saying that name one day. She had sounded nervous.

"How did you know?" Liz asked.

Catherine didn't tell her. "But why take all of this out on *me?*" she asked.

Liz rose again from the sofa to face Catherine. "Because," she said through gritted teeth, "my mother always said she hoped your mother would someday find out what it feels like to lose the person she is closer to than anybody else."

"But that's crazy, Liz." Immediately Catherine regretted using that word.

Liz's eyes blazed. She leapt up to stand right in front of Catherine.

Catherine's heart began whacking again. She strained to catch the ropes holding her hands over the nail head. But it was hopeless. They were just too tight.

"I'm sorry, Liz. I didn't mean that." She took a moment to calm herself down. Was there some way she could distract Liz? "You know," she said, "you really had me fooled. I had no idea it was you doing all those things to me."

The wild look faded from Liz's eyes, and she smiled. "You had no idea, either, that I was smart enough to carry off something like this, did you? That tombstone episode on the tape was nice, wasn't it? And how about the phone call right at the same time as the one on the show? That was a neat bit of planning."

"Yes," Catherine agreed. "How did you do that, Liz?"

"You didn't even think about the fact that

my uncle owns an electronics store," Liz chided. "Bad detective work, Cath. I've learned a lot of stuff from him. Stuff that even Kade would be proud of." She seemed pleased with herself. "I had my camcorder with me for a class project the day we met Travis, the day I decided what I was going to do. I found that soap box in the garbage by the home-ec room and had a brilliant idea about how to start things going."

Catherine thought about what had happened. "But how did you manage to edit in that scene in such a short time?"

"Aha!" Liz paced energetically across the floor. "You don't remember that Kade said he made a backup tape. It wasn't hard to sneak into the electronics room and take the one tape. I merely taped that little scene starring you over part of the episode. I switched tapes in your machine as I rode home with you and Kade that day."

Things were becoming clear to Catherine. "Then you sneaked into my apartment and changed the tapes when I was out screeching for Kade."

Liz chuckled. "It worked out so well, didn't it? I planted that bug on your phone, too. It's inside the mouthpiece where Kade didn't think to look. It was tuned in to a neat little device that started up when I gave it the proper signal. Remember how I clapped my hands just before the phone rang and that message came on?"

"I'm impressed, Liz. The auditorium thing was pretty good, too, and the loose railing at my house." Catherine waited a moment, then said, "What is it you plan to do to me now?"

Liz turned to stare out of the tall window again. "I don't know, Cassandra. We'll find out tomorrow."

Was she calling her "Cassandra" just to tease her, Catherine wondered. Or had Liz finally flipped out totally?

Now Catherine knew she'd been right about what Liz was going to do. She would watch *Lost River* the next day to see what happened to Cassandra. Then the same thing would happen to Catherine.

"We'll find out together," Liz went on. "We'll watch your soap opera and find out how Cassandra — and you — are going to die. The script is already written. There's no way to change it."

"Yes, there is," Catherine said reasonably. "They make changes in scripts all the time."

"Shut up!" Liz yelled. "There won't be any changes in this one."

*   *   *

Catherine got very little sleep that night. Liz fed her a TV dinner she found in the refrigerator. After leading her to the bathroom, she tied her firmly to the sofa and told her to go to sleep.

Catherine wished she'd left her standing there at the post. She'd made a little headway on the knots, sawing them against the protruding nail head when Liz wasn't watching her.

Liz settled down on a small daybed nearby and slept soundly.

The next morning she fixed breakfast, and after they ate she led Catherine back to the sofa.

"Could I stand up awhile, please?" Catherine asked. "It's more comfortable than sitting down, what with my hands and feet being tied."

She was thinking again of that nail on the stair post. Her only hope.

Liz shrugged. "Won't be long now, Cath," she said. "*Lost River* comes on in a couple of hours. If you want to spend your last moments standing, it's all right with me."

She tied Catherine securely to the post.

"Isn't this fun?" she said as she finished. "Waiting to see what your fate will be?"

She laughed, then went over to the sofa where she sat down, humming softly to herself and staring out the window.

It was just a matter of waiting, now. Waiting for that day's episode to begin. Waiting to find out what was going to happen to Cassandra. And to Catherine.

How had the last murder on the show happened? It had been a guy named Drake. Somebody had bashed him with a sledgehammer.

Catherine strained against her bonds. She shouldn't be thinking of things like that. She should be concentrating on those knots.

They didn't seem as tight that morning.

Catherine leaned over a little, hooking the rope over that exposed nail head, the way she'd done the night before. It caught. Cautiously she began sawing it back and forth. It would take a while.

She was careful not to make any noise. She was off to one side of Liz, not directly in her line of sight. If she was really careful, maybe she could undo the knots.

Why didn't somebody come to rescue her? On the soap operas, somebody always burst through the door at the last moment to save a person in peril.

But how would anybody know where she was?

Her mother must be frantic.

"Liz," Catherine said. "My mother has been good to you. You used to say that you wished your mother was more like her."

Liz turned her head slightly, and Catherine stopped her sawing motion.

"Yes, she has been good to me. Maybe she'll let me come live with her after you're gone," Liz said dreamily. "I could have your room. I could have your life, Cassandra."

Liz *had* totally flipped out. No use trying to talk to her.

So Catherine just waited. Waited, and worked on the ropes around her wrists. She got one finger inside a knot and pulled at it. The rope was stiff and rough and she knew she was rubbing the skin right off her finger. But she kept trying, even though it seemed hopeless.

"It's time," Liz said at 11:59.

She turned on the TV. A commercial ended, and the theme music for *Lost River* came on.

Catherine scarcely saw the screen. One of the knots was loosening. Hardly breathing, she worked at it behind her back. If only she could get it undone before something terrible happened to Cassandra.

She looked now at the TV.

The person in the dark, hooded coat was pushing Cassandra past crumbling tombstones. They were in a cemetery. The camera did not show Darkcoat's face.

"Here we are, Cassandra," Darkcoat growled, yanking the bag from Cassandra's head.

Cassandra gasped as she looked at Darkcoat.

At last the camera showed the viewers who it was. Dane Ransom! Cassandra's old boyfriend, the one before Weston Fremont. Long before Dr. Carlton Wyatt.

"Well, what do you know?" Liz said.

Catherine was breathless from working on the stubborn knot, but she smoothed out her voice to ask, "I didn't really suspect Dane, did you, Liz?" She tugged at the knot while she spoke.

Liz gave a short laugh. "I guess it's always the person you least suspect, isn't it, Catherine?"

She seemed to be enjoying this whole thing.

Cassandra glared at Dane. "Why are you doing this to me?"

"If I can't have you, then nobody else can either," Dane snarled.

"I like my reasons better," Liz said. "But then, it's only a soap opera."

"That's right," Catherine said desperately. "It's not real, Liz. It's all just a script. It *can* be rewritten."

"Shut up!" Liz's voice was harsh and she looked around at Catherine as she half-rose from the sofa. "Shut up, Cassandra. I don't want you distracting me."

Cassandra was pleading. "Let me go," she said. "You loved me once, Dane."

"Yes," Dane agreed. "But you left me, Cassandra. It almost killed me." He yanked her over to a crazily tilted gravestone. "So now I'll return the favor. And just to make it all the more interesting, I'll let you dig your own grave. I even brought a rose. A bloodred one, for your funeral."

"Wow," Liz breathed. "Wish I'd thought of that. Wish I'd thought of the grave thing, too." She glanced over at Catherine. "Know of any cemeteries nearby, Cath?" Her eyes glittered.

Catherine shivered.

Dane untied Cassandra's hands. "Just in case you think you can get away, let me tell you I have a gun," he said. "So grab that shovel there and start digging."

There was a shovel leaning against a rough stone that had the initials C.B. carved on it.

Cassandra reached out for the shovel, but just

as her hands touched it she crumpled to her knees.

"Not going to faint, are you, Cassandra?" Dane sneered.

She drooped lower.

Dane walked closer, taking the gun from his pocket.

As he bent down to look at her, Cassandra half-rose and swung the shovel. It slashed Dane's hand, knocking the gun several feet away.

"Hey," Liz said, straightening up. "That's not supposed to happen."

Now Cassandra was on her feet, swinging that shovel again. Dane ducked and tried to look for his gun.

Cassandra was faster than he was. Dropping the shovel, she got to the gun first, but when she bent to get it she accidentally kicked it over against the tombstone that said "C.B."

Dane was bending over now to pick it up. Frantically, Cassandra reached down and grabbed a large hunk of a crumbled gravestone. She raised it up high.

Liz stood up. "No. No. No." She looked around at Catherine, then back at the screen.

Cassandra brought the big piece of stone down on the back of Dane's head with a sickening thunk.

191

Catherine felt the knot she'd been working on loosen. In a second her hands were free. There was still the rope around her feet, but that was tied loosely. It would take only a moment to undo.

"No," Liz whispered again as the scene dissolved into a commercial. Her eyes seemed glued to the screen.

Catherine bent and undid the rope around her feet. Straightening up, she looked frantically around for a weapon. What could she use?

Liz turned her head. "It wasn't supposed to be like that," she whispered. She leapt to her feet when she saw Catherine was free.

Catherine reached out for the only weapon in sight, the spindly telephone table. She grabbed it by one of its long legs, spilling the telephone to the floor with a clatter.

"We have to follow the script, Liz," she said. She raised the little table high above her head and walked toward Liz.

Suddenly Liz darted for the fireplace, and before Catherine could do anything about it, she'd snatched up the poker that stood by its side.

"The show's not over yet, Cath," she said.

Chapter 16

They stood there for what seemed like a long time, each taking stock of the other. Catherine was sure Liz would use the poker if necessary. She wasn't that sure about herself. Could she really swing the little table and hit Liz? The thought of it made her sick.

Swiftly shifting the little table so she was holding it by its top, she pointed its spiky legs at Liz and took a step toward her. Then another step.

Liz's eyes were wild. "Don't come any closer," she said. "I'm bigger than you are, Cath. And this poker can splinter that stupid little table into toothpicks."

"Go ahead," Catherine said calmly. She took another step.

The commercial on the TV was over, and out of the corner of her eye Catherine could see Cassandra standing over Dane's limp body. She bent over him, and as she reached out to feel his pulse his arm moved. He grasped her around the wrist.

"Watch out, Cassandra," Catherine hissed.

Liz's eyes shifted momentarily to the TV screen, but a moment was all Catherine needed. She moved in, shoving that little table in front of her. The legs caught Liz in the chest, knocking her to the floor. The poker fell from her hand, onto the hearthstone.

Catherine bent to grab it. It would make a better weapon than the little table.

Dropping the table, she wrapped both hands around the handle of the poker and raised it high.

Liz just lay there on the floor, rubbing a spot on her neck where one of the table legs had struck her. She looked up at Catherine, and suddenly she smiled.

"Hey, Cath," she said. "Cool it. This has been fun, don't you think? Living a real live soap opera, I mean?" She started to sit up. "Quite an adventure, wouldn't you say?"

Catherine stayed where she was, with the poker raised. "Nice try, Liz. But I'm not buying it. It hasn't been all that much fun for me." She glanced over to where the telephone lay on the floor. "Now, I want you to lie flat and stay real still while I call for help. Don't even start to get up, or I'll whack you."

The concluding music of *Lost River* played on the TV and the credits started to roll. They were leaving Cassandra in peril until the following day.

"You don't know how it's going to come out," Liz said. "He could still kill her, you know."

"Maybe," Catherine admitted. "But I do know how this little scene right here will come out, and so do you." She had backed up to where she could now reach the telephone.

But before she could even bend over, there was a frantic knock at the door.

"Cath," someone yelled, and someone else said, "Cathy, are you in there?"

It was Kade, and Travis, too. They'd come!

Catherine felt weak with relief. She turned to run to the door to let them in. Liz took the opportunity to leap to her feet, charging straight at Catherine.

This was the test. Catherine despaired, thinking there was no way she could actually hit Liz with the heavy poker. The thought of it thudding against human flesh sickened her.

But Liz was upon her.

Cassandra had been able to hit Dane when her life was threatened.

If Cassandra could do it, so could Catherine.

Gritting her teeth, she swung, aiming at Liz's shoulder.

The impact was as sickening as she thought it would be. And it stopped Liz. She fell back to the floor, groaning and clutching her shoulder.

"Stay down," Catherine commanded, raising the poker again.

Breathing heavily, she walked backward over to the door and opened it.

It wasn't until Kade and Travis rushed into the room and grabbed Liz's arms that Catherine let go of the poker. Her hands were so stiff that she practically had to pry them open. The poker clattered to the floor.

"How did you know where to find me?" she said weakly after Liz was subdued and quiet.

"Believe it or not," Travis said, "it was Britny who gave us the clue. We all watched the *Lost River* episode today to see if that would help us any, and we talked about checking the cemeteries nearby. But Britny said that was dumb because Liz wouldn't know that was where Cassandra was being taken until the show came on."

Kade interrupted. "We figured Liz had taken

you because she took Travis's car and didn't bring it back."

"I let her take it," Travis said, shamefaced. "She said you'd run out of the classroom and she wanted to hurry to your place to be with you. I believed her."

"It's okay, Travis," Catherine said.

"The key to the cabin was on my ring," Travis said. "Since Liz had my keys, Britny said that's probably where Liz would take you." He looked at Liz. "Not too swift, going to the cabin, Liz."

Liz didn't answer. Her eyes weren't focused. She was muttering something to herself. Something about Cassandra and Uncle Joe and bloodred roses.

"She needs help," Catherine said. "Let's go."

They called Catherine's mother before heading back to town in Kade's car. They left Travis's car there at the cabin to be picked up later.

"Quite an obsession she had," Travis said as they drove away from the cabin. He was in the backseat with Liz, whose hands were bound.

"Almost as bad as mine," Catherine said, turning to look back at Travis.

He nodded. "We all have our problems. Some of us learn how to handle them."

"Did you learn to handle yours?" she asked gently.

"Yes," Travis said. "I'm all right now, Catherine. Someday I'll tell you about it."

They took Liz to the police station where they waited until she'd been booked and taken away for some kind of evaluation. She was still spaced out, but as she was led away she turned to Catherine and said, "It's still not over, C.B."

Maybe it would never be over. Maybe the effects of what happened to T. J. Jalinsky and Joe Sims would be felt down through yet another generation. It seemed to Catherine that real life was as complicated and tangled as the soap opera plots.

Kade and Travis moved in closer to her. They walked on either side of her as they left the police station and crossed the parking lot to go home.

She was glad they were there. Her two good friends. Being friends with both of them was enough for now.

"Are you going to watch tomorrow's episode of *Lost River?*" Travis asked.

"No," Catherine said emphatically. She shivered.

But if she didn't watch, she'd always wonder if Cassandra got away from Dane Ransom.

That's why she taped the next day's show,

and why she and Kade and Travis hurried to her house after school to watch it.

The show opened where yesterday's episode had left off. Cassandra had just bashed Dane with a big piece of a broken tombstone, and Dane, who appeared to be unconscious, had grabbed her wrist when she bent down to check his pulse.

Frantically, Cassandra reached for another piece of the tombstone, smaller but jagged and sharp. Before Dane could yank her down, she struck him again. Again and again and again. Blood spurted from the cuts the stone made.

This time Dane lay still.

Cassandra stood there over his body, sobbing in quiet terror. "I had to do it, Dane," she whispered. "It was either you or me."

Dane didn't move.

Cassandra hesitated for just a moment. "I've killed him," she whispered to the surrounding graves.

Blindly she ran out of the cemetery.

"So that takes care of him," Catherine said. "Come on out to the refrigerator, guys, and we'll celebrate my triumph over my own private soap opera with a tall glass of Pepsi."

"I'll take you up on that," Travis said.

Both he and Kade followed Catherine out to the kitchen.

But the TV continued to babble on. The scene shifted to one of the other story lines, then the camera came back to the cemetery.

It panned over the tilting old tombstones. It passed Dane's body lying limp and bleeding in the overgrown grass. It went on, then came back to focus on the body.

Dane's hand moved, then a leg. Slowly, painfully, he pulled himself up to his knees, wiping the streaming blood out of his eyes with one hand. His hair was matted with blood and dirt. He stared in the direction Cassandra had gone.

"It's still not over, C.B.," he said.

P●INT CRiME

If you like Point Horror, you'll love Point Crime!

A murder has been committed . . . Whodunnit?
Was it the teacher, the schoolgirl, or the best friend? An exciting new series of crime novels, with tortuous plots and lots of suspects, designed to keep the reader guessing till the very last page.

Also in the *Point Horror* series

THE UNDERWORLD TRILOGY
Peter Beere

When life became impossible for the homeless of London many left the streets to live beneath the earth. They made their homes in the corridors and caves of the Underground. They gave their home a name. They called it UNDERWORLD.

UNDERWORLD
It was hard for Sarah to remember how long she'd been down there, but it sometimes seemed like forever. It was hard to remember a life on the outside. It was hard to remember the real world. Now it seemed that there was nothing but creeping on through the darkness, there was nothing but whispering and secrecy.

And in the darkness lay a man who was waiting to kill her . . .

UNDERWORLD II
"Tracey," she called quietly. No one answered. There was only the dark threatening void which forms Underworld. It's a place people can get lost in, people can disappear in. It's not a place for young girls whose big sisters have deserted them. Mandy didn't know what to do. She didn't know what had swept her sister and her friends from Underworld. All she knew was that Tracey had gone off and left her on her own.

UNDERWORLD III
Whose idea was it? Emma didn't know and now it didn't matter anyway. It was probably Adam who had said, "Let's go down and look round the Underground." It was something to tell their friends about, something new to try. To boast that they had been inside the secret Underworld, a place no one talked about, but everyone knew was there.

It had all seemed like a great adventure, until they found the gun . . .